ALSO BY FERDINAND VON SCHIRACH

Crime

guilt

guilt

STORIES

Ferdinand von Schirach

Translated by Carol Brown Janeway

Alfred A. Knopf · New York · 2012

THIS IS A BORZOI BOOK
PUBLISHED BY ALFRED A. KNOPF

Translation copyright © 2012 by Carol Brown Janeway
All rights reserved. Published in the United States by Alfred A. Knopf,
a division of Random House, Inc., New York, and in Canada by
Random House of Canada Limited, Toronto.
www.aaknopf.com

Originally published in Germany as *Schuld* by Piper Verlag GmbH,
Munich, in 2010. Copyright © 2010 by Piper Verlag GmbH, Munich.

Library of Congress Cataloging-in-Publication Data
Schirach, Ferdinand von, [date]
[Schuld. English]
Guilt : stories / Ferdinand von Schirach ;
[translated by] Carol Janeway.—1st American ed.
p.   cm.
"Originally published in Germany as *Schuld* by
Piper Verlag GmbH, Munich, in 2010"—T.p. verso.
Summary: "A new collection of stories from the critically
acclaimed author of CRIME"—Provided by publisher.
ISBN 978-0-307-59949-0 (hardback)
1. Guilt—Fiction. 2. Innocence (Psychology)—Fiction.
3. Responsibility—Fiction. I. Title.
PT2720.I73S3813 2012
833'.92—dc23   2011024227

Jacket design by Barbara de Wilde

Manufactured in the United States of America
First American Edition

Things are as they are.

—Aristotle

CONTENTS

Funfair 3

DNA 13

The Illuminati 19

Children 37

Anatomy 45

The Other Man 49

The Briefcase 63

Desire 71

Snow 75

The Key 87

Lonely 111

Justice 117

Comparison 121

Family 135

Secrets 141

guilt

Funfair

The first of August was too hot, even for the time of year. The little town was celebrating its six-hundredth anniversary, the air smelled of candied almonds and candy floss, and greasy smoke rose from the grills to settle in people's hair. There were all the stands you usually find at annual fairs: a carousel had been put up, you could go on the bumper cars or shoot an air gun. The older people spoke of "the Emperor's weather" and the "dog days," and wore bright-colored pants and open shirts.

They were respectable men with respectable jobs: insurance salesman, car dealer, skilled carpenter. You would have no cause to find fault with them. Almost all of them were married, they had children, they paid their taxes, their credit was good, and they watched the news on television every evening. They were perfectly normal men, and nobody would have believed that something like this could happen.

They played in a brass band. Nothing exciting, no big events, Queen of the Grape Harvest, annual Rifle Club outing, Fire Department picnic. They had once played for the president of the Republic, out in his garden; there had been cold beer and sausages afterwards. The photo now hung in their meeting hall; the head of state himself was nowhere to be seen, but someone had stuck the newspaper article up next to it to prove it was all real.

They sat on the stage with their wigs and their fake beards. Their wives had made up their faces with white powder and rouge. The mayor had said that everything was to look dignified today "in honor of the town." But things didn't look dignified. They were sweating in front of the black curtain and they'd had too much to drink. Their shirts were sticking to their bodies, the air smelled of sweat and alcohol, and there were empty glasses between their feet. They played nonetheless. And if they hit false notes it didn't matter because the audience had drunk too much too. In the pauses between the pieces they played there was applause and more beer. When they took a break, a radio announcer acted as a DJ. The wooden floor in the front of the curtain was giving off clouds of dust because people were dancing despite the heat, so the musicians went back behind the curtain to drink.

The girl was seventeen and still had to ask permission at home if she wanted to stay the night at her boyfriend's. In a year she would sit her school-leaving exams, then she would be off to study medicine in Berlin or Munich. She was looking forward to it. She was pretty, with blue eyes and an open face, and she laughed as she served the drinks. The tips were good; she wanted to travel across Europe with her boyfriend during the summer vacation.

It was so hot that she was only wearing a T-shirt with her jeans, and sunglasses, and a green hair band. One of the musicians came out in front of the curtain, waved at her, and pointed to the glass in his hand. She crossed the dance floor and climbed the four steps up to the stage, balancing the tray that was too heavy for her small hands. She thought the man looked funny with his wig and his white cheeks. He smiled, she remembered that; he smiled and his teeth looked yellow against the white of his face. He pushed the curtain aside, letting her into where the other men were sitting on two benches, all thirsty. For a moment her white T-shirt gleamed with an odd, bright flash in the sun; her boyfriend always liked it when she wore it. Then she slipped. She fell backwards, it didn't hurt, but the beer spilled all over her. Her T-shirt became transparent; she wasn't wearing a bra. She felt embarrassed, so she laughed, and then she looked at the men, who had suddenly gone silent and were staring at her. The first man reached out a hand towards her, and it all began. The curtain was closed again, the loudspeakers were blaring a Michael Jackson song, and the rhythm on the dance floor became the rhythm of the men, and later nobody could explain anything.

The police came too late. They didn't believe the man who'd called from the public phone booth. He'd said he was one of the band but didn't give his name. The policeman who took the call told his colleagues, but they thought it was a joke. Only the youngest of them thought he should maybe take a look, and went across the street to the fairground.

It was dark and dank under the stage. She was lying there naked in the mud, wet with sperm, wet with urine, wet with blood. She couldn't speak, and she didn't move. She had two broken ribs, a broken left arm, and a broken nose; splinters from the glasses and the beer bottles had gashed her back and arms. When the men had finished, they had lifted one of the boards and thrown her under the stage. They had urinated on her as she lay down there. Then they had gone out front again. They were playing a polka as the policemen pulled the girl out of the muck.

———

"Defense is war, a war for the rights of the accused." The sentence appeared in the little book with the red plastic cover that I always carried around with me back then. It was the *Defense Attorney's Pocket Reference.* I had just sat my second set of exams and been admitted to the bar a few weeks earlier. I believed in that sentence. I thought I knew what it meant.

A friend I had studied with called up to ask me if I'd like to work with him on a defense; they still needed two lawyers. Of course I wanted to; it was a big case, the papers were full of it, and I thought this was going to be my new life.

In a trial, no one has to prove his innocence. No one has to defend himself; only the prosecutor has to provide proofs. And that was also our strategy: all of them were simply to keep silent. We didn't have to do anything more than that.

DNA analysis had only recently been admitted at trial. The policemen had secured the girl's clothing at the hospital and stuffed it into a blue garbage bag. They put the bag in the trunk of their patrol car, to be delivered to the medical examiner. They thought they were doing everything right. The car stood in the sun for hour after hour, and the heat caused fungi and bacteria to grow under the plastic wrapping; they altered the traces of DNA and no one could analyze them any more.

The doctors saved the girl, but destroyed the last of the evidence. As she lay on the operating table, her skin was washed. The traces the perpetrators had left in her vagina, her rectum, and on her body were rinsed away; nobody was thinking of anything except her emergency care. Much later the police and the medical examiner from the state capital tried to locate the waste from the operating room. At some point they gave up: at 3 a.m. they sat in the hospital cafeteria in front of pale brown cups of filtered coffee; they were tired, and had no explanations. A nurse told them they ought to go home.

The young woman couldn't name her attackers; she couldn't tell one from another; under the makeup and the wigs they all looked alike. At the lineup she didn't want to look, and when she did manage to overcome her aversion, she couldn't identify any of them. Nobody knew which of the men had called the police, but it was clear that it had been one of them. Which meant that any one of them could have been the caller. Eight of them were guilty, but each of them could also be the one innocent party.

He was gaunt. Angular face, gold-framed glasses, prominent chin. At that time, smoking was still permitted in the visitors' rooms in prisons; he smoked one cigarette after the other. As he was talking, spittle built up in the corners of his mouth which he wiped away with a handkerchief. He had already been detained for ten days when I saw him for the first time. The situation was as new for me as it was for him; I gave him too elaborate an explanation of his rights and the relationship between lawyer and client, too much textbook knowledge as a form of insecurity. He talked about his wife and his two children, about his work, and finally about the Funfair. He said it had been too hot that day and they'd drunk too much. He didn't know why it had happened. That was all he said—it had been too hot. I never asked him if he'd joined in; I didn't want to know.

The lawyers were staying in the hotel on the town's market square. In the taproom we discussed the file. There were photos of the young woman, of her maltreated body, of her swollen face. I had never seen anything like this. Her statements were confused, they gave us no clear picture, and on every page of the file you could read fury, the fury of the policemen, the fury of the DA, the fury of the doctors. None of it did any good.

In the middle of the night, the phone rang in my room. All I could hear was the caller's breathing; he didn't say a word.

Funfair

He hadn't dialed a wrong number. I listened to him until he hung up. It took a long time.

———

The court was on the same square as the hotel, a classical building with a small flight of steps in front, a celebration of the might of the law. The town was famous for its winepresses, merchants, and the winegrowers who lived there; it was a blessed piece of land, sheltered from all wars. Everything radiated dignity and upright behavior. Someone had planted geraniums on the window ledges of the court.

The judge called us into his room one by one. I wore a robe, because I didn't know you don't wear robes to such meetings. When the review of the remand in custody began, I talked too much, the way you talk when you're young and you think anything's better than saying nothing. The judge only looked at my client; I didn't think he even listened to me. But something else was standing between the judge and the man, something much older than our code of legal procedure, an accusation that had nothing to do with the laws as written. And when I had finished, the judge asked once again if the man wished to remain silent. He asked quietly, with no inflection in his voice, while he folded up his reading glasses and waited. The judge knew the answer, but he asked the question. And all of us in the cool air of the courtroom knew that the legal proceedings would end here and that guilt was another matter entirely.

———

Later we waited out in the hall for the examining magistrate to render his decision. We were nine defense lawyers; my friend and I were the youngest. The two of us had bought new suits for this hearing. Like all lawyers we were exchanging jokes; we didn't want the situation to get the better of us, and now I was one of them. At the end of the hall a sergeant was leaning against the wall; he was fat and tired and he despised every one of us.

That afternoon the judge vacated the warrant; he said there was no proof, the accused had remained silent. He read out the decision from a sheet of paper, although it was only two sentences long. After that, everything was still. The defense had been the right one, but now I didn't know if I should stand up until the woman recording the court proceedings gave me the decision and we left the room. The judge could have rendered no other verdict. The hall outside smelled of linoleum and old files.

The men were released. They left by a rear exit and went back to their wives and children and their lives. They paid their taxes and kept their credit good, they sent their children to school, and none of them spoke of the matter again. But the brass band was dissolved. There was never a formal trial.

———

The young girl's father stood in front of the court; he stood in the middle of the flight of steps as we went past to right and left; nobody touched him. He looked at us, red-eyed from weeping. It was a good face. The town hall opposite still had a poster advertising the anniversary celebration. The older lawyers spoke to the journalists, the microphones glittered like fish in the sun; behind them the father sat down on the courthouse steps and buried his head in his arms.

———

After the remand hearing, my study partner and I went to the station. We could have talked about the defense victory or about the Rhine right there next to the rail tracks, or about anything at all. But we sat on the wooden bench with its peeling paint, and neither of us felt like saying a word. We knew we'd lost our innocence and that this was irrelevant. We remained silent as we sat in the train in our new suits with our barely used attaché cases beside us, and as we journeyed home, we thought about the girl and the respectable men, and we didn't look at each other. We had grown up, and when we got out, we knew that things would never be simple again.

DNA

For M.R.

Nina was seventeen. She sat outside the subway station at the zoo, a paper cup with a few coins in it in front of her. It was cold; there was already snow on the ground. She hadn't imagined things would be this way, but it was better than any alternative. The last time she had phoned her mother had been two months ago, and her stepfather had answered. He had cried and told her she should come home. And it all came back to her: his sweaty old man's smell, his hairy hands. She hung up.

Her new friend Thomas also lived in the station. He was twenty-four, and he looked after her. They drank a lot, the hard stuff that warmed you up and let you forget everything. When the man came toward them, she thought he was a john. She wasn't a prostitute and she got furious if men asked her how much it cost. One time she spat in someone's face.

The old man asked her to come with him, he had a warm apartment, and he didn't want sex. He just didn't want to be alone at Christmas. He looked respectable, he was maybe sixty or sixty-five, thick overcoat, polished shoes. The shoes were always the first thing she checked. She was freezing.

"Only if my friend can come too," she said.

"Of course," said the man; in fact he'd like that even better.

Later they sat in the man's kitchen. There was coffee and cake. The man asked if she'd like to take a bath, it would do her good. She felt uneasy, but Thomas was there. Nothing can happen, she thought. The bathroom door had no key.

She lay in the bathtub. It was warm and the bath oil smelled of birches and lavender. She didn't see him at first. He had closed the door behind him, dropped his trousers, and was masturbating. It was nothing serious, he said, smiling uncertainly. She could hear the television in the other room. She screamed. Thomas pushed the door open and the handle caught the man in the kidneys. He lost his balance and fell over the edge of the bathtub. He landed next to her in the water, his head on her stomach. She lashed out, pulled her knees up, trying to get out, away from the man. She hit him on the nose, and blood ran into the water. Thomas grabbed him by the hair and held him under the surface. Nina was still screaming. She stood up in the bath, naked, and helped Thomas by pressing on the man's neck. It's taking time, she thought. Then he stopped moving. She saw the hairs on his ass and punched his back.

"Swine," said Thomas.

"Swine," said Nina.

They didn't say anything more after that; they went into the kitchen and tried to think clearly. Nina had wrapped a towel around her. They smoked. They had no idea what to do.

Thomas had to get her things out of the bathroom. The man's body had slid onto the floor and was blocking the door.

"You know they're going to have to lever the door off its hinges with a screwdriver?" he said in the kitchen as he handed her her clothes.

"No, I didn't."

"Otherwise they won't get him out."

"Will they manage?"

"It's the only way."

"Is he dead?"

"I think so," he said.

"You have to go back in. My wallet and my identity card are still in there."

He searched the apartment and found 8,500 deutschmarks in the desk. It said "For Aunt Margret" on the envelope. They wiped away their fingerprints, then left the apartment. But they were too slow. The neighbor, an elderly woman with strong glasses, saw them in the arcade.

They took the suburban train back to the station. Later they went to a snack bar.

"It was terrible," said Nina.

"The idiot," said Thomas.

"I love you," she said.

"Yes."

"What is it? Do you love me too?"

"Was he the only one doing something?" asked Thomas, looking straight at her.

"Yes. What are you thinking?" Suddenly she was afraid.

"Did you do something too?"

"No, I screamed. The old swine," she said.

"Absolutely nothing?"

"No, absolutely nothing."

"Things are going to get tough," he said after a pause.

A week later they saw the poster on a pillar in the station. The man was dead. A policeman knew them from the squad room in the station. He thought the neighbor's description might fit them, and they were taken in for questioning. The old lady wasn't sure. Adhesive tests were done on their clothing and compared to fibers from the dead man's apartment. The results were inconclusive. The man was recognized as a john; he had two previous convictions for sexual assault and intercourse with minors. They were released. The case remained unsolved.

———

They had done everything right. For nineteen years they had done everything right. Using the dead man's money they had rented an apartment; later they moved into a row house. They had stopped drinking. Nina was a salesgirl in a supermarket; Thomas worked as the stores supervisor at a wholesaler. They had gotten married. Within the year she'd given birth to a boy, and then twelve months later a girl. They made their way; things went well. Once he got into a fistfight at the company. He didn't defend himself; she understood.

When her mother died, she relapsed. She started smoking marijuana again. Thomas found her at the station, in her old spot. They sat on a bench in the Tiergarten for a couple of hours, then drove home. She laid her head in his lap. She didn't need it any more. They had friends and were close to his aunt in Hannover. The children were doing well in school.

———

When the science had advanced sufficiently, the cigarettes in the dead man's ashtray underwent molecular genetic analysis. All those who had been under suspicion back then were summoned for a mass screening. The document looked threatening: a shield, the inscription "President of Police of Berlin," thin paper in a green envelope. It lay on the kitchen table for two days before they could bring themselves to talk about it. There was no avoiding it; they went, nothing more than a cotton swab in the mouth, it didn't hurt.

A week later they were arrested. The chief commissioner said, "It's better for you." He was only doing his job. They admitted everything, they didn't think it mattered any more. Thomas called me too late. The court could not have ruled out an accident if they had kept quiet.

———

Six weeks later they were released from custody. The examining magistrate said the case was utterly unusual, the accused had integrated themselves fully into society in the meantime. They were under the gravest suspicion and a conviction was certain, but they were not a flight risk.

———

guilt

No one ever found out where the gun came from. He shot her in the heart and himself in the temple. Both of them died immediately. A dog discovered them the next day. They were lying on the shore of the Wannsee, side by side, sheltered in a sand pit. They hadn't wanted to do it in the apartment; they'd painted the walls only two months before.

The Illuminati

The Order of the Illuminati was founded on May 1, 1776, by Adam Weishaupt, an instructor in canon law at the University of Ingolstadt. Only the students of the Jesuits had access to the libraries, and Weishaupt wanted to change this. The professor had no organizational talent; perhaps at the age of twenty-eight he was simply too young. Adolph von Knigge, a Freemason, took over the leadership of the secret society in 1780. Knigge knew what he was doing; the Order grew until it began to pose a threat to the Crown because of its sympathy for the ideas of the Enlightenment, and this finally led to both him and it being banned as enemies of the state. After that, theories abounded. Because Adam Weishaupt looked a little like George Washington, it was claimed that the Illuminati had murdered the president and replaced him with Weishaupt—for Weishaupt means whitehead and the national symbol of the United States, the white-headed or bald eagle, was proof of this. And because people loved conspiracy theories even back then, suddenly everyone became a member of the Illuminati: Galileo, the Babylonian goddess Lilith, Lucifer, and eventually even the Jesuits themselves.

In reality, Weishaupt died in 1830 in Gotha; the history

of the Order ended with its ban by the government in 1784, and all that remains is a small memorial tablet in the pedestrian precinct in Ingolstadt.

For some people, that's not enough.

———

When Henry was six he was sent to school and things began to go wrong. The goody cone he was given to celebrate his first day was made of red felt with stars stuck on it and a magician with a pointy beard. It was a heavy cone, it had a green paper cover, he'd carried it all by himself since they'd left the house. Then the cone got caught on the door handle of the classroom and that made a dent in it. He sat on his chair and stared at his cone and everyone else's cones, and when the teacher asked his name, he didn't know what he was supposed to say and he began to cry. He was crying because of the dent, because of the strange people, because of the teacher, who was wearing a red dress, and because he'd pictured everything differently. The boy next to him stood up and went in search of a new neighbor. Until that moment Henry had thought the world had been created for him; sometimes he had turned round quickly, hoping to catch objects as they changed places. Now he would never do that again. He remembered nothing about the rest of the lesson, but later he believed his life had been knocked out of balance that day in a way that could never be righted again.

Henry's parents were ambitious; his father was the kind of man that no one in their little town ever saw without a tie and polished shoes. Despite all the strains created by his background, he had become the deputy director of the power company and a member of the town council. His wife was the daughter of the richest farmer in the area. And because Henry's father had only had ten years of school, he wanted more for his son. He had a false picture of private schools, and he mistrusted state schools, which is why the parents decided to enroll Henry in a boarding school in southern Germany.

———

An allée lined with chestnut trees led to the former sixteenth-century monastery. The school board had bought the building sixty years before; it had a good reputation. Industrialists, top officials, doctors, and lawyers sent their children here. The headmaster was a fat man with a cravat and a green jacket; he greeted the family at the big front door. His parents talked to the unknown man as Henry walked behind them, looking at the leather patches on the man's elbows and the reddish hairs on his neck. His father's voice was softer than usual. Other children came from the opposite direction; one of them nodded to Henry but he didn't want to respond and looked at the wall. The unknown man showed them Henry's room for the next year; he'd be sharing it with eight other boys. The beds were bunk beds, and there was a linen curtain in front of each one. The man told Henry this was now his "kingdom"; he could stick posters up with Scotch tape. He said this as if he were being friendly. Then he slapped him on the shoulder. Henry didn't understand him. The unknown man's hands were soft and fleshy. Finally he went away.

guilt

His mother packed everything into his cupboard. It was all strange; the sheets and pillowcase had nothing to do with home and all the noises sounded different. Henry was still hoping it was all a mistake.

His father was bored. He sat next to Henry on the bed and both of them watched as Henry's mother unpacked the three suitcases. She talked without pause, saying she wished she'd been to a boarding school, and she'd loved holiday camps when she was young. The singsong in her voice made Henry feel tired. He leaned against the head of the bed and closed his eyes. When he was awoken, nothing had changed.

A fellow pupil came and said he'd been told to "show the parents around." They saw two classrooms, the dining room, and the kitchenette; everything dated from the seventies, the furniture had rounded corners, the lamps were orange, it was all comfortable and nothing looked as if it belonged in a monastery. His mother was enchanted by everything, and Henry knew how stupid the other pupil thought she was. At the end, his father gave the boy two euros. It was too little, and his mother called him back and gave him more. The boy bowed, holding the money in his hand, and looked at Henry, and Henry knew he'd already lost.

At some point his father said it was late already and they still had the long return drive ahead of them. As they headed down the allée, Henry saw his mother turning back towards him one more time and waving. He saw her face through the window and he saw her saying something to his father; her red mouth moved silently, it would move forever, and he suddenly grasped that it wasn't moving for him any more. He kept his hands in his pockets. The car got smaller and smaller until he could no longer distinguish it from the shadows in the allée.

He was twelve years old now and he knew that all this was premature and much too serious.

———

The boarding school was a world unto itself, more constricted, more intensive, devoid of compromise. There were the athletes, the intellectuals, the showoffs, and the winners. And there were the ones who were ignored, who were mere wallpaper. No one made his own decision as to who he was, it was the others who judged and their judgment was almost always final. Girls could have provided the corrective, but the school didn't admit them, so their voices were missing.

Henry was one of the inconspicuous ones. He said the wrong things, he wore the wrong clothes, he was bad at sports, and he couldn't even play computer games. No one expected anything of him, he was one of the ones who went along, people didn't even make fun of him. He was also one of the ones no one would recognize at future class reunions. Henry found a friend, one of the boys in his dorm room, who read fantasy novels and had wet hands. In the dining hall they sat at the table that got served last, and they stuck together on class outings. They got through, but when Henry lay awake at night, he wished there were something more for him.

He was an average student. Even when he really tried, it made no difference. When he turned fourteen he developed acne, and everything got worse. The girls he met in his little town during the vacations wanted nothing to do with him. If they bicycled to the quarry pond on summer afternoons, he had to pay for the ice cream and the drinks in order to be allowed to sit with them. And in order to be able to do this, he stole money from his mother's wallet. The girls kissed other boys all the same, and all he had left at night were the drawings he had made of them secretly.

Things went differently only once. She was the prettiest girl in the clique; it was during the summer vacation when he had just turned fifteen. She had told him he should come with her, just like that. He had followed her into the cramped changing cubicle; it was a wooden shed by the lake with a narrow bench and no window, full of junk. She undressed in front of him in the semi-darkness and told him to sit down and unzip his pants. The light coming in between the planks divided her body; he saw her mouth, her breasts, her pubic hair, he saw the dust in the air and smelled the old inflatable mattresses under the bench, and he heard the others by the lake. She knelt in front of him and took hold of him; her hands were cold and the light fell on her mouth and her teeth, which were too white. He felt her breath in front of his face, and suddenly he was afraid. He sweated in the dark little room as he stared at her hand that was holding his penis and the veins on the back of her hand. He suddenly thought of an excerpt from their biology textbook: "the fingers of a hand open and close themselves 22 million times in the course of a life." He wanted to touch her breasts but he didn't dare to. Then he got a cramp in his calf, and as he came, because he had to say something he said, "I love you." She jumped to her feet and turned away; his stomach was sticky with sperm. Bending over, she pulled her bikini back on hastily, then opened the door and turned back towards him as she stood in the doorway. He could see her eyes now. They held sympathy and disgust and something else he didn't yet recognize. Then she said "Sorry" softly and slammed the door, running to join the others out of sight. He sat in the dark for a long time. When they met next day, she was standing among her friends. She said loudly, for everyone to hear, that he shouldn't stare at her so idiotically; she'd lost a bet, that was all, and "that thing yesterday" had been the stake. Because he was young and vulnerable, the imbalance grew even more severe.

———

In ninth grade a new teacher arrived at the boarding school; she taught art and suddenly Henry's life changed. Up until then school had been a matter of indifference to him; he'd have been happier doing something else. Once during a vacation he'd done an apprenticeship in a screw factory back home. He'd like to have stayed there. He enjoyed the orderly course of things, the unchanging rhythm of the machines, the unchanging nature of the conversations in the cafeteria. He liked the foreman he was assigned to, who answered his questions in monosyllables.

Everything changed with the new teacher. There were a handful of drawings in his parents' house, quick sketches made for tourists which his father had bought from fly-by-night dealers in Paris during their honeymoon. The only original came from Henry's grandfather and hung over the bed in his boyhood room. It was of a summer landscape in East Prussia; Henry could feel the heat and the loneliness and he knew for sure, though he had no grounds for it, that it was a good picture. At school he had drawn figures for his friend out of the fantasy novels; there were scenes with dwarves, orcs, and elves, and the way Henry drew them gave them more life than the language in the books did.

The teacher was almost sixty-five years old and came from Alsace. She wore black-and-white suits. Her upper lip wobbled a little when she talked about art, and that's when you could hear the faint remaining traces of her French accent.

As always at the beginning of the school year, she had the children paint a scene from their vacations. That afternoon she leafed through their work, to see how far along they were. As she took the pictures out of the folder one by one, she was smoking, something she only did at home. From time to time she made notes. Then she held Henry's sheet of paper in her hands. It was a drawing, just a few pencil strokes, of his mother collecting him at the station. She hadn't so much as noticed the boy in class, but now her hand began to tremble. She understood his drawing, it was all evident to her. She saw the struggles, the wounds, and the fear, and suddenly she saw the boy himself. That evening, her entry in her diary consisted of two sentences: "Henry P is the greatest talent I have ever seen. He is the greatest gift of my life."

―――

They caught him shortly after Christmas vacation.

An indoor swimming pool had been built on to the monastery in the 1970s. It was muggy in there, and smelled
of chlorine and plastic. The boys used the anteroom to
change. Henry had hurt his hand on the edge of the pool
and was allowed to leave ahead of the others. A few minutes
later another boy went to fetch his watch; he wanted to mea-
sure how long they could stay underwater. As he came into
the anteroom, he saw Henry taking money out of the other
boys' pants, counting it and hiding it away. He watched him
for several minutes, while the water dripped onto the tiled
floor. At a certain point Henry noticed him and heard him
say "You swine." Henry saw the puddle of water beneath the
boy's feet, his green-and-white swimming trunks, and his
wet hair that hung down into his face. Suddenly the world
slowed, he saw a single drop falling in slow motion, its surface perfect, the neon light on the ceiling refracting itself
within it. As it splashed onto the floor, Henry did something he shouldn't have done and which later he couldn't
explain to anyone: he knelt. The other boy grinned down at
him and repeated, "You swine, you're going to pay for this."
Then he went back to the swimming pool.

―――

The boy belonged to a little group in school who secretly
called themselves the Illuminati. During his summer vacation he had read a book about defunct orders, the Templars

and the Illuminati. He was sixteen and seeking explanations for the world. He gave the book to the others and after a few months they knew all the theories. There were three of them; they talked about the Holy Grail and world conspiracies, they met at night, searched for signs in the monastery, and finally they found symbols because they wanted to find them. The arches of the windows threw midday shadows that looked like pentagrams; they discovered an owl, the emblem of the Illuminati, in the dark portrait of the abbot who had founded the monastery; and they thought they saw a pyramid above the clock on the tower. They took it all seriously, and because they talked to nobody about it all, things took on an unfounded significance. They ordered books on the Internet, they went onto innumerable websites, and gradually they came to believe what these said.

When they arrived at exorcism, they decided to seek out a sacrificial victim, someone they could purify of his sins and make their disciple. Much later, after everything had happened, more than four hundred books were found in their cupboards and night stands, books on Inquisition trials, Satanic rituals, secret societies, and flagellants, and their computers were full of images of the torturing of witches and sadistic pornography. They thought a girl would be ideal and they talked about what they would do with her. But when the thing with Henry happened at the swimming pool, the die was cast.

———

The teacher was careful with Henry. She let him draw what he wanted. Then she showed him pictures; she explained anatomy to him, and perspective and composition. Henry sucked it all in; none of it gave him any difficulties. He waited every week for the two hours of art class. When he had made some progress, he took his sketch pad outdoors. He drew what he saw, and he saw more than other people did. The only person the teacher talked to about Henry was the headmaster; they decided to let Henry continue to grow within the shelter provided by the school; he still seemed overly fragile. He began to grasp the pictures in the art books, and he slowly realized that he was not alone.

———

For the first few weeks they humiliated him in a haphazard way. He had to polish their shoes and buy candy for them in the village. Henry did what they told him. Then came the carnival holiday before Lent; the boys had three days off, as every year, but for most of them it was too far to go home. They were bored, and things for Henry got worse. The monastery had an outbuilding; during the monks' time it had been the slaughterhouse. There were two rooms inside, with yellow tiles that reached all the way to the ceiling. It had stood empty for many years, but the old chopping blocks were still there, as were the drainage channels for blood in the floor.

He was made to sit naked on a chair, while the three boys circled round him screaming that he was a swine and a thief and a traitor to their community, and human garbage, and ugly. They talked about his acne and his penis. They beat him with wet towels. He was only allowed to move if he was on his knees, or they made him crawl on his stomach; and he had to keep repeating "I have brought great guilt upon myself." They forced him into an iron butcher's barrel and banged on the metal until he almost went deaf. And they discussed what they should do with the pathetic creature. Shortly before supper, they stopped. They were friendly to him and told him to get dressed again; they would continue next weekend but for now they mustn't be late for supper.

That evening one of them wrote home about how the week had gone, and that he was looking forward to the holidays. He mentioned his marks in English and mathematics. The two others played soccer.

Henry went back to the slaughterhouse again after supper. He stood in the half-darkness and waited, but he didn't know what he was waiting for. He saw the streetlamp through the window, he thought about his mother and how he'd once eaten chocolate in the car and smeared it on the seat. When she discovered this, she got very angry. He spent the whole afternoon cleaning the car, not just the seats but the exterior too; he even scrubbed the tires with a brush, till the car gleamed and his father complimented him. And then suddenly he took off his clothes, lay down on the floor, and spread his arms wide. He felt the cold rising up into his bones from the flagstones. He closed his eyes and listened to nothing except his own breath. Henry was happy.

———

"He ascended into heaven and sitteth at the right hand of God the Father Almighty. From thence he shall come to judge the quick and the dead . . ."

It was the liturgy for Good Friday; attendance at the vil-

lage church was compulsory for the boys. Originally it had
been a Lady Chapel; now it was a baroque church full of gold,
trompe l'oeil marble, angels and Madonnas.

Henry had long since drawn everything that was in here,
but today he saw nothing. He groped for the piece of paper
in his pocket. *"Hodie te illuminatum inauguramus,"* it said. "Today
we will consecrate you as one of the Illuminati." He had
waited for it, the piece of paper meant everything to him,
he'd found it this morning on his night table. Under the
Latin text it said, "8 pm. Old Slaughterhouse."

". . . and forgive us our trespasses . . ."

"Yes," he thought, "today my trespasses will be forgiven."
He was breathing so loudly that a couple of the boys turned
round to look at him. They were already in the middle of the
Lord's Prayer, the liturgy would end at any moment. "My
trespasses will be forgiven," he said half out loud, and closed
his eyes.

———

Henry was naked and was made to put the noose around
his neck himself. The others were wearing black hoods that
they had found in a forgotten cupboard in the attic, rough
monk's robes and penitent's shirts made of goat hair which
hadn't been worn in modern times. They had placed candles around, and the flames were reflected in the grimy film
on the windows. Henry could no longer recognize the boys'
faces, but he saw all the details: the fabric of the hoods, the
thread the buttons were sewn on with, the red bricks of the
window frames, the forced lock in the door, the dust on
the steps, the rust on the banisters.

guilt

They bound his hands behind his back. Using watercolors from art class, one of the boys painted a red pentagram on Henry's chest to ward off evil; they'd seen it in some engraving. They took the rope around his neck and pulled it up to a hook in the ceiling using the old winch; Henry's toes could barely touch the floor. One of the boys read out the great exorcism, the Rituale Romanum, the papal instructions written in Latin in 1614. His words rang out in the room; nobody understood them. The boy's voice cracked; he was being carried away by himself. They really believed they were purifying Henry of his sins.

Henry didn't freeze. This time, this one time, he'd done everything right; they could no longer reject him. One of the boys swung at him with a whip he'd made himself, with knots in the leather. It wasn't a hard blow, but Henry lost his balance. The rope was made of hemp; it cut into his throat and blocked his air passages, he tripped, his toes could no longer find the floor. And then Henry got an erection.

A person being slowly hanged suffocates. In the first phase the rope cuts into the skin, the veins and arteries in the neck are closed off, and the face turns violet-blue. The brain is no longer supplied with blood, consciousness is lost after about ten seconds; only if the windpipe is not totally blocked does it take longer. In the next phase, which lasts approximately one minute, the breathing muscles contract, the tongue protrudes from the mouth, and the hyoid bone and the larynx are damaged. This is followed by powerful, uncontrollable cramps; the legs and arms thrash eight or ten times, and the neck muscles often tear. Then suddenly the hanged man seems peaceful, he's no longer breathing, and after one or two minutes the last phase begins. Death is now almost inevitable. The mouth opens, the body gasps for air, but only in individual panting spasms, no more than ten in sixty seconds. Blood may issue from the mouth, nose, and ears, the face is now congested, the right ventricle of the heart is distended. Death comes after approximately ten minutes. Erections during a hanging are not uncommon: in the fifteenth century people believed the mandrake, a solanaceous herb, grew from the sperm of hanged men.

But the young men knew nothing about the human body. They didn't understand that Henry was dying; they thought the blows were arousing him. The boy with the whip became furious, he struck harder and roared something that Henry didn't understand. He felt no pain. He remembered finding a deer on a country road as a child that had been hit by a car. It was lying there in its own blood in the snow, and when he tried to touch it, it jerked its head round and stared at him. Now he was one of them. His trespasses had been wiped away, he would never be alone again, he was purified, and finally he was free.

———

The road from the art teacher's house to the only gas station in the village ran between the monastery and the old slaughterhouse. She wanted to buy cigarettes there, and set off on her bike. She saw the light from the candles in the slaughterhouse and knew that no one was allowed to be there. She had been a teacher her whole life, she had supervised children and brought them up; it was probably this sense of responsibility that made her stop and climb the five worn steps. She opened the door. She saw the candles, she saw Henry, naked with a stiff penis, half-hanged in the noose, and she saw the three boys in their monk's hoods, one of them with a whip in his hand. She screamed, backed away, missed the stair, lost her balance, and hit the nape of her neck on the edge of the bottom step. Her neck snapped and she died immediately.

The rope round Henry's neck was made fast to an iron chain that ran over a pulley in the ceiling and then to the winch. When he heard the teacher scream, the boy let go, the rope gave way, and Henry fell to the floor. The heavy chain raced over the pulley, yanking the plaster off the ceiling, and its weight shattered a flagstone next to Henry's head. While the boys ran into the school to fetch help, Henry lay there, then he slowly pulled in his knees, breathed, and when he opened his eyes, he saw the teacher's purse lying overturned in the doorway.

———

The headmaster had been put in touch with me by the school's lawyer. He told me what had happened and asked me to represent the interests of the school. He knew the teacher had had a particularly close relationship with Henry, closer than with any of the other pupils, and although he'd always trusted her, he was now worried that her death might have something to do with this.

———

When I reached the school five days after the events, the old slaughterhouse was still blocked off with red-and-white crime tape. The DA said the investigating authorities had no cause to suspect the art teacher. The detectives found her diary. I exercised my right to review the file, and read it in my hotel room.

Then there were the pictures. The police found them in Henry's cupboard. He had recorded it all, rapid watercolor sketches on hundreds of sheets of paper; every humiliation was there, every humiliation of his and every desire of his torturers. The pictures would become the main evidence at trial; no one would be able to deny a thing. Not one of the sketches showed the art teacher; her death really had been an accident. I wasn't able to speak to Henry, who had been taken home, but there were almost fifty pages of interview transcripts, and I talked to his friend for many hours.

By the end of the week I was able to reassure the head-master. Henry's parents were not going to sue the school; they didn't want their son's case to become public knowledge. The DA's office didn't intend to put the school administration on trial. The criminal action against the students would not be a public one; they were just seventeen, and the only issue would be their guilt. My brief mandate was thus at an end.

A lawyer who was a friend of mine and was defending one of the young men told me later that they had all confessed and had been sentenced to three years in juvenile detention. They had not been charged with the death of the teacher.

guilt

———

Some years afterwards, when I was in the neighborhood, I phoned the headmaster and he invited me to coffee at the monastery. The old slaughterhouse had been torn down and was now a parking lot. Henry had not returned to the school. He was ill for a long time and now works in the screw factory where he had already served his apprenticeship. He has never gone back to drawing.

That evening I drove back down the same allée along which Henry had been driven to the school by his parents so many years before. I saw the dog too late. I braked and the car skidded on the gravel road. The dog was huge and black; it took its time crossing the road and didn't even look at me. In the Middle Ages such dogs were supposed to pull mandrake roots out of the ground; people believed the plants would scream when dug up and the scream would kill people. The dogs obviously didn't mind. I waited until it disappeared between the trees.

Children

Before they came to take him away, things had always gone well for Holbrecht. He had met Miriam at a supper given by friends. She was wearing a black dress and a silk shawl with brightly colored birds of paradise on it. She taught at the primary school; he was the sales representative for an office furniture company. They fell in love, and after that time was over they still got along well together. At family parties, everyone said they made such a good-looking couple, and most of them meant it.

A year after the wedding they bought a semi-detached house in one of the most respectable suburbs of Berlin, and five years later they had almost paid it off. "Ahead of time," as the local branch manager of the Volksbank said. He always stood up when he saw Miriam or Holbrecht at the counter. Holbrecht liked that. There's nothing to find fault with, he thought.

Holbrecht wanted children. "Next year," said Miriam. "Let's enjoy life a little longer." She was twenty-nine, he was nine years older. They were going to take a trip to the Maldives that winter, and whenever they talked about it, Miriam looked at him and smiled.

Customers valued his straightforward manner; when his bonus was added in, he was making a comfortable ninety thousand a year. Driving back from meetings, he listened to jazz in the car, and his world was complete.

———

They came at seven in the morning. He'd been supposed to drive to Hannover that day: a new customer, complete equipping of an office, good contract. They handcuffed him and led him out of the house. Still in her pajamas that he liked so much, Miriam stared at the arrest warrant. "Twenty-four counts of child abuse." She knew the name of the girl from her primary school class. She stood in the kitchen with an officer as two of the policemen led Holbrecht down the narrow path to the police car. They had planted the box-wood hedge the year before; the jacket she'd given him last Christmas hung awkwardly on his shoulders somehow. The policeman said most wives had no idea. It was meant to sound comforting. Then they searched the house.

———

It wasn't a long trial. Holbrecht denied everything. The judge held up the fact that porno films had been found on his computer. Admittedly there were no children in them and the films were legal, but the women were very young: one of them had barely any tits. The judge was sixty-three. He believed the girl. She said Holbrecht had always inter-cepted her on the way home. He had touched her "down there"—she started to cry as she testified about that. The ter-race of his house was where it took place. Another girl confirmed everything; she'd even seen it all twice herself. The girls described the house and the little garden.

Miriam didn't attend the main hearing. Her lawyer sent the divorce papers to the house of detention. Holbrecht signed everything without reading it.

The court sentenced him to three and a half years. It stated in its opinion that it had no cause to doubt the girl's testimony. Holbrecht served out his sentence to the last day. The psychologist had wanted him to acknowledge his guilt. He said nothing.

———

His shoes were soaked by the rain; water had forced its way in over the rims and seeped into his socks. The bus shelter had a plastic roof, but Holbrecht preferred to stand outdoors. The rain ran down the back of his neck into his coat. Everything he owned fit into the gray suitcase that was standing beside him. Some underwear, a few books, approximately 250 letters to his wife which he had never sent. In the pocket of his pants he had the addresses of his probation officer and a boardinghouse where he could stay to begin with. To tide him over, he had the money he'd earned in prison. Holbrecht was now forty-two years old.

The next five years passed quietly. He lived on his wages as a sandwich-board man for a tourist restaurant. He stood at the end of the Kurfürstendamm with colorful pictures of the various pizzas on cardboard boxes. He wore a white hat.

His trick was to give a little nod to people when he handed them the flyer. Most of them took one.

He lived in a one-and-a-half-room apartment in Schöneberg. His employer valued him; he was never ill. He didn't want to live on unemployment benefits and he didn't want any other job.

———

He recognized her at once. She must now be sixteen or seventeen, a carefree young woman in a close-fitting T-shirt. She was with her boyfriend, eating ice cream. She tossed her hair back as she laughed. It was her.

He turned aside quickly, feeling ill. He pulled off the sandwich board and told the restaurant owner he was sick. He was so pale that no one asked him any questions.

In the suburban train someone had written "I love you" and someone else had written "pig" in the dirt on the window. Back home he lay down on his bed in his clothes, and spread a wet kitchen towel over his face. He slept for fourteen hours. Then he got up, made coffee, and sat down at the open window. A shoe was lying on the canopy of the building next door. Children were trying to reach it with a stick.

In the afternoon he met his friend, a homeless man, who was fishing in the Spree, and sat down beside him.

"It's about a woman," said Holbrecht.

"It's always about a woman," said his friend.

Then they fell silent. When his friend pulled a fish out of the water and killed it by smacking it against the concrete wall of the quay, he went home.

Back in the apartment he looked out of the window again. The shoe was still lying on the canopy. He fetched a beer from the refrigerator and pressed the bottle to his temples. The heat had barely eased at all.

———

She had walked by him and his sandwich board on the Kurfürstendamm every Saturday. He took the weekend off and waited. When she came he followed her; he waited in front of shops and cafés and restaurants. Nobody noticed him. On the fourth Saturday she bought movie tickets. He found a seat directly behind her. His plan was going to work. She had put her hand on her boyfriend's thigh. Holbrecht sat down. He smelled her perfume and heard her whispering. Pulling the kitchen knife out of the waistband of his pants, he clutched it under his jacket. She had pinned her hair up; he saw the blond fuzz on the back of her slender neck. He could almost count the individual tiny hairs.

He thought he had every right.

———

I don't know why Holbrecht came straight to my office. I have no walk-in clients, but the office is not far from the movie house: maybe that's the only reason. My secretary called me early in the morning; a man was waiting without an appointment, he'd been sitting on the steps outside the office, and he had a knife. My secretary has been with me for years. Now she was afraid.

Holbrecht sat hunched in a chair, staring at the knife in front of him on the table. He didn't move. I asked him if I might take the knife. Holbrecht nodded without looking up. I put it in an envelope and carried it to the secretary's office. Then I sat down with him and waited. At some point he looked at me. The first thing he said was "I didn't do it." I nodded; sometimes it's hard for clients to talk. I offered him a coffee, then we sat there and smoked. It was midsummer, and through the large open windows of the conference room you could hear high voices—children on a class outing. Young people were laughing in the café across the way. I closed the window. It was quiet and warm.

It took a long time before he told me his story. He had a strange way of talking: He nodded after every sentence, as if he had to personally reaffirm everything he said. And there were long pauses. At the end he said he'd followed the girl into the movie house but he hadn't stabbed her; he couldn't bring himself to do it. He was trembling. He had sat all night in front of my offices and he was exhausted. My secretary called the movie house: there had been no incident.

———

Next day Holbrecht brought the documents from the old trial. The young woman's address was in the phone book. I wrote to her and asked if she would talk to me. It was the only possibility we had. I was surprised when she actually showed up.

She was young, training in the hospitality business. Freckled, nervous. Her boyfriend came with her. I asked him to wait in another room. When I told her Holbrecht's story, she went quiet and looked out the window. I told her we couldn't win the right to a new hearing unless she testified. She didn't look at me, and she didn't answer. I wasn't sure if she would help Holbrecht, but when she held out her hand to say goodbye, I saw that she had been crying.

———

A few days later, she mailed me her old diary. It was pink, with horses and hearts printed on the cloth cover. She had started to write it a few years after the events; it really had a grip on her. She had stuck yellow Post-its on some of the pages for me. She had come up with the whole plan when she was eight. She wanted to have Miriam, her teacher, all to herself: she was jealous of Holbrecht, who sometimes came to pick up his wife. It was a little girl's fantasy. She had persuaded her girlfriend to back up her story. That was all.

A new trial was granted, the girlfriend admitted what the two of them had done back then, and Holbrecht was exonerated at the new hearing. It wasn't easy for the young women to testify. They apologized to Holbrecht in open court. He didn't care. We managed to keep the press out of it. He was awarded damages for the time he'd spent in prison as an innocent man. They amounted to a bit more than thirty thousand euros.

guilt

———

Holbrecht bought a little café in Charlottenburg; it sells homemade chocolates and good coffee. He lives with an Italian woman who loves him. Sometimes I drink an espresso there. We never discuss the affair.

Anatomy

He sat in the car. He had fallen asleep briefly, not a deep sleep, just a dreamless nodding-off for a few seconds. He waited and drank from the bottle of schnapps he'd bought in the supermarket. The wind blew sand against the car. The sand was everywhere here, a few centimeters under the grass. He was familiar with it all; he'd grown up here. At some point she would come out of the house and walk to the bus stop. Maybe she'd be wearing a dress again, a thin one, preferably the one with yellow and green flowers on it.

He thought about how he'd spoken to her. About her face, her skin under her dress, about how tall she was and how beautiful. She had barely looked at him. He had asked if she would like something to drink. He wasn't sure if she'd understood. She'd laughed at him. "You're not my type," she'd yelled, because the music was too loud. "I'm sorry," she added. He'd shrugged, as if it didn't matter. And grinned. What else was he supposed to do? Then he'd gone back to his table.

She wasn't going to make fun of him today. She would do what he wanted. He would possess her. He imagined her fear. The animals he'd killed had felt fear as well. He'd been able to see it. They smelled different just before they died. The larger they were, the more fear they felt. Birds were boring. Cats and dogs were better; they knew when death was coming. But animals couldn't talk. She would talk. It would be crucial to do it slowly so as to get the most out of it. That was the problem. Things mustn't move too fast. If he was too excited, it would go wrong. The way it did with the very first cat. He'd lost control right after he'd amputated the ears, and he'd stabbed it convulsively much too soon.

The set of dissecting instruments had been expensive, but it was complete, including bone shears, a Stryker saw to split open the skull, the knife for cutting through cartilage, and the knife for severing the head. He'd ordered it on the Internet. He knew the anatomical atlas almost by heart. He'd written everything down in his diary, from the first meeting in the nightclub until today. He'd taken photos of her secretly and glued her head onto pornographic pictures. He'd drawn in the line where he wanted to cut, with black dashes, like in the anatomical atlas.

She came out of the front door, and he got ready. As she shut the garden door behind her, he climbed out of the car. This would be the hardest part. He had to compel her to come with him, but she mustn't cry out. He had written down all the possible variants. Later the police found the notes, the pictures of the young woman, the slaughtered animals, and hundreds of splatter films in his parents' cellar. The officers had searched the house when they found his diary and the dissecting tools in his car. He also had a small chemistry lab in the cellar—his attempts to make chloroform had been unsuccessful.

The right side of the Mercedes hit him as he got out of his car. He flew over the hood, slammed his head onto the windshield, and landed on the ground on the left side of the car. He died on the way to the hospital. He was twenty-one.

I defended the driver of the Mercedes. He got an eighteen-month suspended sentence for negligent homicide.

The Other Man

Paulsberg stood next to his car. As he did every evening, he had turned off on the way home and driven up the little hill to his old ash tree. He had often sat here as a child in the shadow of the branches, carving figures out of wood and playing hooky. He lowered the window; the days were already getting shorter again and the air was cooler. It was quiet. For the only moment in the day. His cell phone was switched off. From here he could see his house, the house where he had grown up, built by his grandfather. It shone brightly, the trees in the garden lit by the sun; he could see the cars parked by the road. He would be there in a few minutes, his guests would already be waiting, and he would have to talk about all the idiocies that go to make up social life.

Paulsberg was forty-eight now. He owned seventeen major retail businesses in Germany and Austria that sold expensive men's clothing. His great-grandfather had established the knitwear factory back there in the valley; Paulsberg had already learned everything about fabric and cut when he was a child. He had sold the factory.

He thought about his wife. Slim, elegant, enchanting, she would make conversation with everyone. She was thirty-six, a lawyer in an international firm, black suit, hair loose.

guilt

He had met her in the airport in Zurich. They had both been waiting for their delayed flight in the coffee bar and he'd made her laugh. They made a date. Two years later they got married. That was eight years ago. Things could have gone well.

But then the thing in the hotel sauna happened, and it changed everything.

———

Every year since their marriage, they had spent a few days in a mountain hotel in Upper Bavaria. They liked this way of unwinding, sleeping, walking, eating. The hotel was much cited for its "wellness environment." There were steam baths and Finnish saunas, indoor and outdoor pools, massages and mud packs. The garage was full of Mercedeses, BMWs, and Porsches. Everyone belonged.

Like most men of his age, Paulsberg had a paunch. His wife had kept herself in better shape. He was proud of her. As they sat in the sauna he observed the young man staring at her. A southerner, black hair, Italian perhaps, good-looking, smooth skin, tanned, around twenty-five. The stranger was looking at his wife as if she were some beautiful animal. It irritated her. He smiled at her; she looked away. Then he stood up with his penis half-erect, walked towards the exit, and stopped in front of her, turning so that his member was right in her face. Paulsberg was about to intervene when the young man wrapped a towel around his hips and nodded to him.

Later, when they were back in their room, they made jokes about it. They saw the stranger at dinner; Paulsberg's wife smiled at him and blushed. They talked about him for the rest of the evening, and during the night they imagined what it would be like with him. They had sex for the first time in a long time. They were afraid, and they were turned on.

Next day at the same time they went back to the sauna, and the stranger was already waiting there. She opened her towel while she was still at the door, and walked slowly past him, naked, knowing exactly what she was doing and wanting him to know too. He got to his feet and stood in front of her again. She sat on the bench, and looked first at him, then at Paulsberg. Paulsberg nodded and said "Yes" in a loud voice. She took the stranger's penis in her hand. Paulsberg saw the rhythmic motions of her arm through the steam in the sauna, he saw the young man's back in front of his wife, olive-skinned and shining wet. Nobody spoke; he heard the stranger panting; the movements of his wife's arm became slower. Then she turned to Paulsberg and showed him the stranger's sperm on her face and body. The stranger picked up his towel and left the sauna without saying a word. They stayed behind in the heat.

———

First they experimented in public saunas, then in swinger clubs, and finally they advertised on the Internet. They established rules: no violence, no love, no encounters at home. They would stop it all if either of them started to feel uncomfortable. They never stopped once. At the beginning he was the one who wrote the copy, then she took over; they posted masked photos on websites. After four years they had it down to a science. They'd found a discreet country hotel. There they would meet men on weekends who'd answered their ads. He said he was making his wife available. They thought it was a game, but after so many encounters it wasn't a game any more, it had become a part of them. His wife was still a lawyer, she was still radiant and unapproachable, but on weekends she became an object used by other people. That was how they wanted it. It had simply presented itself; there was no explanation.

———

The name in the e-mail had meant nothing to him, nor could he connect the photo with anyone; he had stopped looking at the photos the men sent a long time ago. His wife had written back to the man and now he was standing in front of them in the hotel reception area. Paulsberg knew him fleetingly from school thirty-five years before. They had had nothing to do with each other there. He was in the parallel class. They sat on the barstools in the lobby and told each other the things people who've been at school together always tell each other; they talked about former teachers, the friends they'd both known, and tried to ignore the situation. But it didn't get any better. The other man ordered whiskey instead of beer and spoke too loudly. Paulsberg knew the firm he worked for; he was in the same business. The three of them ate dinner together, and the other man drank too much. He flirted with Paulsberg's wife, saying she was young and beautiful and Paulsberg was to be envied, and he kept on drinking. Paulsberg wanted to leave. She began to talk about sex and about the men who sent her pictures and whom they met. At a certain point she laid her hand on the other man's hand, and they went to the room they always booked.

While the other man was having sex with his wife, Paulsberg sat on the sofa. He looked at the picture that hung over the bed: a young woman standing on the seashore. The artist had painted her from behind, in a blue-and-white bathing suit of the kind worn back in the twenties. She must be beautiful, he thought. At some point she would turn around, smile at the artist, and they would go home together. Paulsberg thought about the fact that they had been married for eight years now.

Later, when they were alone in the car, neither of them said a word. She stared out of the passenger window into the darkness until they reached home. During the night he went to the kitchen to drink a glass of water, and when he came back he saw the display on her phone light up.

She had been taking Prozac for a long time. She thought she was dependent on it and never left the house without the green-and-white pills. She didn't know why she satisfied men. Sometimes in the night, when the house was still and Paulsberg was asleep and she couldn't stand the bright green numbers on her alarm clock, she got dressed and went out into the garden. She would lie down on one of the lounge chairs by the pool and look up at the sky, waiting for the feeling that she'd known ever since her father died. She could hardly bear it. There were billions of solar systems in the Milky Way and billions of Milky Ways. And in between, nothing but cold and the void. She had lost control.

———

Paulsberg had long since forgotten about the other man. He was at the annual association conference in Cologne, standing at the buffet in the breakfast room, when the man called his name. Paulsberg turned around.

Suddenly the world slowed down and became viscous. Later he would remember every image, the butter floating in ice water, the colorful yogurt cartons, the red napkins and the slices of sausages on the white hotel plates. Paulsberg thought the other man looked like one of those blind amphibians he'd seen as a child in caves in Yugoslavia. He'd caught one once back then, and carried it all the way back to the hotel, wanting to show his mother. When he opened his hand, it was dead. The other man's head was shaved bald; watery eyes, thin eyebrows, thick lips, almost blue. The lips had kissed his wife. The other man's tongue moved in slow motion, pushing against the inner surface of his front teeth as he said his name. Paulsberg saw the colorless threads of spittle, the pores on his tongue, the long thin hairs in his nostrils, the larynx pressing hard against the reddened skin from the inside. Paulsberg didn't understand what the other man was saying. He saw the girl in the blue-and-white bathing suit from the picture in the hotel; she turned around towards him, smiled, then pointed to the thin man kneeling over his wife. Paulsberg felt his heartbeat stop; he imagined himself falling over, dragging the tablecloth down with him. He saw himself lying dead between the sliced oranges, the white sausages, and the cream cheese. But he didn't fall. It was only a moment. He nodded at the other man.

———

There were all the usual speeches at the association meeting. They looked at presentations, and there was filter coffee out of silver vacuum jugs. After a few hours nobody was listening any more. It was nothing special.

That afternoon the other man came to his room. They drank the beer he'd brought with him. He also had some cocaine and offered Paulsberg a line; he tipped the powder onto the glass table and inhaled it through a rolled-up banknote. When he went to the bathroom to wash his hands, Paulsberg followed him. The other man was standing at the basin, bent over to wash his face. Paulsberg saw his ears and the yellowed edge of his white shirt collar.

He couldn't help himself.

Now Paulsberg was sitting on the bed. The hotel room was like a thousand others he had slept in. Two slabs of chocolate in the brown minibar, vacuum-packed peanuts, yellow plastic bottle opener. A smell of disinfectant, liquid soap in the bathroom, the sign on the tiles saying please support the environment by reusing your towels.

He closed his eyes and thought about the horse. He had

walked across the bridge that morning and then to the stone steps leading to the water meadows by the Rhine in the early mist that was rising from the river. And suddenly there it was, right in front of him, steam coming off its coat, its nostrils soft and bright red.

He would have to call her at some point. She would ask him when he was coming back. She would tell him about her day, the people in the office, the cleaning lady who banged around the garbage cans too noisily, and all the other things that made up her life. He would say nothing about the other man. And then they would hang up and try to go on with their lives.

Paulsberg heard the other man in the bathroom, groaning. He threw the cigarette into a half-full glass of water, took his traveling bag, and left the room. When he was paying his bill at reception, he said it would be a good idea for the room to be made up quickly. The girl behind the counter looked at him, but he didn't say anything else.

They found the other man twenty minutes later. He survived.

——

Paulsberg had done it with the ashtray in the bathroom.

It was a 1970s piece, thick and heavy, made of dark smoked glass. The medical examiner later categorized it as blunt-force trauma; the edges of the wounds could not be clearly distinguished. The ashtray was identified as the weapon.

Paulsberg had seen the holes in the other man's head as the blood poured out of them, brighter than he had expected.

He's not dying, he thought as he kept hitting the skull. He's bleeding but he's not dying.

Paulsberg finally jammed the other man in between the bathtub and the toilet and laid him facedown on the toilet lid. He'd wanted to hit him one last time, and raised his arm to strike. The other man's hair had clumped together; it looked stiff with blood, black wires like pencils on the pale skin of his head. Suddenly Paulsberg found himself thinking about his wife, and the way they'd said goodbye for the first time, in January ten years ago; the sky was made of ice and they'd stood on the road outside the airport, freezing. He thought of her thin shoes in the slush, and of her blue coat with the big buttons, and the way she'd turned up the collar, holding the lapels together with one hand. She'd laughed; she was lonely and beautiful and wounded. After she'd got into the taxi, he'd known she belonged to him.

Paulsberg set the ashtray down on the floor. The officers found it later among the red smears on the tiles. The other man had groaned quietly again as he left. Paulsberg no longer wanted to kill him.

———

The trial began five months later. Paulsberg was accused of attempted murder. According to the prosecutor, he'd tried to kill the man from behind. The indictment stated that cocaine was at issue. The prosecutor couldn't have known better.

Paulsberg gave no reason for his act and said nothing about the other man. "Call my wife" were his only words to the policeman after his arrest. Nothing more. The judges were looking for a motive. Nobody simply batters another man in his hotel room. The prosecutor had been unable to find any connection between the men. The psychiatrist said Paulsberg was "absolutely normal"; no drugs were found in his system and nobody believed he'd tried to kill out of sheer bloodlust.

The only person who could have provided the information was the other man. But he kept silent too. The judges couldn't force him to testify. The police had found cocaine in his pocket and on the glass table; preliminary proceedings had been initiated against him, and this allowed him to remain silent—he could have incriminated himself by making any statement.

Of course judges do not have to know the motives of a defendant in order to be able to sentence him. But they want to know why people do what they do. And only when they understand can they punish the defendant in a way that is commensurate with his guilt. If that understanding is lacking, the sentence will almost always be longer. The judges didn't know that Paulsberg wished to protect his wife. She was a lawyer; he had committed a crime. Her office had not yet fired her: no one can do anything about an insane husband. But the partners in the law firm would not be able to accept the truth about all the unknown men, and so she would have been unable to continue in her job. Paulsberg left the decision up to his wife. She was to do what she thought was right.

———

She appeared as a witness without legal counsel. She seemed fragile, too delicately spun a creature to belong with Paulsberg. The presiding judge instructed her that she had the right to remain silent. Nobody believed anything new was going to come out now in this trial. But then she started to speak and it all changed.

In almost every jury trial there is this one moment when everything suddenly becomes clear. I thought she was going to talk about the unknown men. But she told a different story. She spoke for forty-five minutes without interruption, she was clear, explicit, and did not contradict herself. She said she had had an affair with the other man and Paulsberg had found out. He had wanted to separate; he was crazed with jealousy. The guilt was hers, not his. She said her husband had found the film she and her lover had made. She handed the bailiff a DVD. Paulsberg and she had often made similar films. This one came from the encounter with the other man. The video camera had been on a tripod next to the bed. The public was asked to leave, as we had to view it. You can find such films on countless sites on the Internet. There was no doubt: it was the other man who was having sex with her. The prosecutor observed Paulsberg while the film was running. He remained calm.

The prosecutor had made yet another mistake. Our criminal law is over 130 years old. It is an intelligent law. Sometimes things don't go the way the perpetrator wants. His revolver is loaded. He has five bullets. He approaches a woman, he shoots, he wants to kill her. He misses four times, only a single shot grazes her arm. Then he's standing right in front of her. He pushes the barrel of the revolver against her stomach, he cocks it, he sees the blood running down her arm, and he sees her fear. Perhaps he has second thoughts. A bad law would sentence the man for attempted murder; an intelligent law wants to save the woman. Our criminal code says that he can step back from his attempt to murder without incurring punishment. Which is to say: if he stops now, if he doesn't kill her, his only punishment will be for endangering her by inflicting bodily injury—not for attempted murder. So it's up to him: the law will be friendly to him if he does the right thing at this point and lets his victim live. Professors call this "the golden bridge." I never liked this expression. The things that go on inside people at such moments are too complicated, and a golden bridge belongs more in a Chinese garden. But the idea behind the law is right.

Paulsberg had stopped beating in the other man's skull. At the end, he no longer wanted to kill him. This meant that he stepped back from attempted murder; the judges could only convict him of endangering someone by inflicting bodily injury.

The court could refute neither Paulsberg's statement nor his wife's testimony; hence it could not refute his motive. He was sentenced to three and a half years.

His wife visited him regularly in prison, then he was transferred to the daytime release program. Two years after the trial the remainder of the sentence was commuted to probation. She resigned her position in the law firm and they moved back to the town where she'd grown up in Schleswig-Holstein; she opened a small law practice there. He sold his shops and the house and began to take photographs. Not long ago he had his first exhibition in Berlin. All the photos were of a faceless naked woman.

The Briefcase

The police sergeant was standing in a parking lot on the Berlin ring road. She and her colleagues were the last checkpoint in a routine traffic control operation, a boring job, and she would have preferred to be one of the drivers sitting in the warmth, only having to open their windows a crack. It was sixteen degrees; only the occasional frozen blade of grass broke through the crusted snow cover, and the damp cold crawled through her uniform and into her bones. She wished she were up at the front, choosing which cars would be checked, but that job belonged to her seniors. She had only moved from Cologne to Berlin two months before. Now she was longing for her bathtub. She just couldn't take the cold; it had never been as bad as this in Cologne.

The next vehicle was an Opel Omega, silver-gray, Polish license plates. The car looked well cared for, no dents, all its lights in order. The driver lowered the window and handed out his license and registration. Everything seemed normal, he didn't smell of alcohol, and his smile was friendly. The policewoman didn't know why, but she had a strange feeling. While she read his papers she tried to identify it. At the police academy they had taught her to trust her instincts, but she had to find a logical reason for them.

It was a rental car from an international company; the rental agreement was made out to the driver and all the papers were right there. And then she realized what was irritating her: the car was empty. There was nothing lying in it, no crumpled chewing gum paper, no newspapers, no suitcase, no cigarette lighters, no gloves, nothing. The car was as empty as if it had just been delivered from the factory. The driver spoke no German. She waved over a colleague who spoke a little Polish. They told the man, who was still smiling, to get out of the car and asked him to open the trunk. The driver nodded and pressed the button. Everything in here was clean to the point of sterility too; the only thing lying in the middle was a briefcase made of red imitation leather. The policewoman pointed to it and made a sign to the man to open it. He shrugged and shook his head. She bent forward to look at the locks. They were simple combination locks, set to zero, and opened immediately. She lifted the lid of the case, and recoiled so violently that she banged the back of her head against the lid of the trunk. She managed to turn away, then she threw up on the road. Her colleague, who hadn't seen what was in the case, drew his weapon and yelled at the driver to put his hands on the roof of the car. Other policemen came running and the driver was overpowered. The policewoman was white; traces of vomit clung to the corners of her mouth. She said, "Oh my God," and then she threw up again.

———

The policemen took the man to the Keithstrasse, which houses the Major Case department. The red briefcase was sent to Forensics. Although it was Saturday, a call was made to Lanning, the chief medical examiner. The briefcase contained eighteen color Xeroxes of corpses, all apparently laser prints. All of their faces looked the same: mouths wide open, eyeballs protruding. People die, and medical examiners deal with them; it's their job. But the pictures were unusual: eleven men and seven women were all lying on their backs in the same twisted pose. When photographed, they had all looked strangely similar: they were naked and the rough point of a wooden stake was sticking out of their stomachs.

———

Jan Bathowitz was the name on the Polish passport. When he was brought in, they wanted to question him at once; the police interpreter was standing ready. Bathowitz was polite, almost submissive, but he kept repeating he wanted to call his embassy first. It was his right and finally they allowed him to make the call. He said his name and the legal staff at the embassy advised him to remain silent until a lawyer could get there. That too was his right, and Bathowitz exercised it.

Chief Inspector Pätzold could hold the suspect until the end of the following day, and this he did. So the man was taken to the holding pen and locked in a cell. As they did with every prisoner, they took away his shoelaces and his belt in case he tried to hang himself. When I got there at two o'clock the next day, the questioning could proceed. I

advised Bathowitz not to answer. Nonetheless he wanted to
testify.

"Your name?" Chief Inspector Pätzold looked bored, but
he was wide awake. The interpreter translated every question and every answer.

"Jan Bathowitz."

Pätzold went through the man's particulars; he had had
the passport checked out and it appeared to be genuine. A
message had been sent to the Polish authorities yesterday,
asking if there were any charges against Bathowitz, but as
always such inquiries took forever.

"Mr. Bathowitz, you know why you're here."

"Your police brought me here."

"Yes. Do you know why?"

"No."

"Where did you get the photos?"

"What photos?"

"We found eighteen photos in your briefcase."

"It's not my briefacse."

"Aha. So whose is it?"

"A businessman from Witoslaw, my hometown."

"What's the name of this businessman?"

"I don't know. He gave me the briefcase and said I was to
bring it to Berlin."

"But you have to know what his name is."

"No, I didn't have to know that."

"Why?"

"I met him in a bar. He spoke to me, he paid me right up
front and in cash."

"Did you know what's in the photos?"

"No, the briefcase was closed when I got it. I have no idea."

"You didn't look inside?"

"It was shut."

"But it wasn't locked. You could have looked inside."

"I don't do things like that," said Bathowitz.

"Mr. Pätzold," I said, "what is the actual charge against my client?"

Pätzold looked at me. That was the point, and of course he knew it.

"We've had the photographs examined. Professor Lanninger says the corpses are most likely genuine."

"Yes?" I said.

"What do you mean, *yes*? Your client had photos of corpses in his briefcase. Corpses with stakes through them."

"I still haven't found out what the charge is. Transporting color Xeroxes of photographs of corpses made by a laser printer? Lanning is no Photoshop expert, and 'most likely' is not the same as 'definitely.' And even if they were genuine corpses, there is no law against having pictures of them. There's nothing here that constitutes a criminal offense."

Pätzold knew I was right. Nonetheless, I could understand him.

At that moment, we could have left. I stood up and took my briefcase. But then my client did something I didn't understand. He laid a hand on my forearm and said he didn't mind the chief inspector's questions. I wanted a break, but Bathowitz shook his head and said, "It's fine."

Pätzold's questions continued. "To whom does the briefcase belong?"

"The man in the bar."

"What were you supposed to do with it?"

"I already said I was supposed to bring it to Berlin."

"Did the man say what was in the case?"

"Yes, he did."

"What?"

"He said it was blueprints for a big project. There was a
lot of money involved."

"Blueprints?"

"Yes."

"Why didn't he send the plans by courier?"

"I didn't ask. He said he didn't trust couriers."

"Why?"

"He said couriers in Poland are always working for both
sides. He preferred to have a stranger whom nobody knew
transport the things."

"Where were you to take the pictures?"

Bathowitz didn't hesitate for a second. He said, "To
Kreuzberg."

Pätzold nodded; he seemed to have reached his goal.

"To whom in Kreuzberg? What's his name?"

I don't understand Polish, but I understood the tone in
Bathowitz's voice. He was totally calm. "I don't know. I was
supposed to go to a phone booth at five o'clock."

"Excuse me?"

"Mehringdamm, Yorckstrasse." He said these words first
in German, then in Polish. "There's apparently a phone

booth there. I'm to be there at five o'clock tomorrow afternoon, and the phone will ring, and I'll be told the rest
of it."

Pätzold continued questioning him for another hour.
The story didn't change. Bathowitz remained friendly, he
answered every question politely, nothing made him tense.
Pätzold couldn't refute any of his statements.

Bathowitz was fingerprinted and photographed. The
computer had no trace of him. The inquiry to Poland
was answered: everything appeared to be in order. Pätzold must either release Bathowitz or go before a judge.
The DA declined to make a request for an arrest warrant;
Pätzold had no choice. He asked Bathowitz if he'd agree
to leave the briefcase with the police. Bathowitz shrugged;
all he asked was a receipt for it. At seven that evening he
was allowed to leave the police station. He said goodbye to
me on the steps of the old building, walked to his car, and
disappeared.

———

Twenty policemen were posted around the phone booth
next day and the police cars in the neighborhood were on
alert. A Polish-born plainclothes officer who had roughly
the same build as Bathowitz and was wearing similar clothes
stood in the phone booth at 5 p.m. with the red briefcase.
A judge had granted a warrant to tap the phone line. The
phone didn't ring.

———

guilt

A jogger found the body on Tuesday morning at a parking spot in the woods. The 6.35-millimeter Browning had made only small entry wounds, circular, barely half a centimeter across. It was an execution. Pätzold could only start a new file and notify his colleagues in Poland. Bathowitz's death was never solved.

Desire

She had positioned the chair in front of the window. She liked to drink her tea there, because she could see into the playground. A girl was doing cartwheels while two boys watched. The girl was a little older than the boys. When she fell down, she started to cry. She ran to her mother and showed her the scrape on her elbow. The mother had a bottle of water and a handkerchief and swabbed the wound clean. The girl looked over to the boys as she stood between her mother's legs holding out her arm to her. It was Sunday. He would be coming back with the children in an hour. She would set the table; friends were coming to visit. It was silent in the apartment. She stared into the playground again without seeing what was happening there.

They were well. She did everything the way she'd always done it: conversations with her husband about work, shopping in the supermarket, tennis lessons for the children, Christmas with her parents or parents-in-law. She uttered the same sentences she always uttered; she wore the same clothes she always wore. She went to buy shoes with her girlfriends, and went to the movies once a month if she could get a babysitter. She kept up-to-date with exhibitions and plays. She watched the news, read the political section of the paper, paid attention to the children, attended parent-teacher days at school. She didn't do any sports, but she hadn't put on weight.

Her husband suited her; she'd always believed that. But it wasn't his fault. It was nobody's fault. It had just happened. She hadn't been able to do anything about it. She could remember every detail of the evening when it all became clear.

"Are you ill?" he had said. "You look pale."

"No."

"What's the matter?"

"Nothing, darling, I'm just going to go to bed now. It was a long day."

Much later, when they were lying in bed, she'd suddenly been unable to breathe. She'd lain awake until morning, rigid with anxiety and guilt, her thighs cramping. She didn't want it that way, but it had stayed that way. And while making breakfast for the children next day and checking their schoolbags, she'd known she'd never feel any different again: she was totally empty inside. She would have to keep living with that.

That had been two years ago. They went on living together; he didn't notice. Nobody noticed. They rarely had sex, and when they did, she was affable with him.

Gradually everything disappeared, until she was a mere shell. The world became alien to her; she no longer belonged in it. The children laughed, her husband got excited, their friends argued—but nothing touched her. She was serious, she laughed, she cried, she comforted—it was all the way it usually was and all on cue. But when things were quiet and she looked at other people in cafés or on the streetcar, she felt none of it had anything to do with her any more.

At some point she started. She stood for half an hour in front of the shelves with the stockings, went away, came back. Then she grabbed. It didn't matter what size or what color. She shoved the packs under her coat too hastily and the stockings slid to the floor. She bent down, then ran. Her heart was racing, she could feel the pulse in her neck and stains on her hands. Her whole body was wet. She didn't feel her legs, she was trembling, then she was past the check-out. Someone bumped into her. Then the ice-cold evening air, and rain. Adrenaline flooded through her; she wanted to scream. Two corners further on, she threw the stockings into a garbage can. Taking off her shoes, she ran home in the rain. Outside her front door she looked up into the sky. The water splashed onto her forehead, her eyes, her mouth. She was alive.

She only ever stole superfluous things, and she only ever stole when she couldn't stand it any longer. She wouldn't always get away with it, she knew that. Her husband would say that was in the nature of things. He always uttered remarks like that. He was right. When the detective stopped her, she immediately confessed, right there on the street. People passing by stopped to stare at her, a child pointed and said, "That woman stole things." The detective was holding her tight by the arm. He took her to his office and wrote up a report for the police: name, address, identity card number, sequence of events, value of goods 12.99 euros, check the relevant box "admitted: yes/no." He was wearing a checked shirt and smelled of sweat. She was the woman with the Louis Vuitton handbag and the Gucci wallet, credit cards, and 845.36 euros in cash. He showed her where to sign. She read the sheet and wondered for a moment if she could correct his spelling mistakes, the way she did with her children. He said she would get something from the police in the mail, and grinned at her. The remains of a sausage roll were lying on the table. She thought of her husband, and imagined the trial, with the judge questioning her. The detective took her out through a side door.

The police asked her to make a written statement. She came to my office with it. It didn't take long to settle. It was the first time, the value of the goods was minimal, she had no previous convictions. The DA stopped the proceedings. No one in the family learned of it.

Things settled down, the way everything in her life had always settled down.

Snow

The old man stood in the kitchen and smoked. It was August, the day was warm, and he'd opened the window wide. He looked at the ashtray: a naked mermaid with a green fishtail and underneath, in script, "Welcome to the Reeperbahn." He didn't know where he'd got it. The color on the girl had faded and the "R" of Reeperbahn had disappeared. The drops of water splashed into the metal sink, slow and hard. It calmed him. He would remain at the window, smoking and doing nothing.

The special task force had assembled in front of the building. The policemen were wearing uniforms that looked too big, and black helmets; they carried transparent shields. They were brought in when things got too difficult for the others, and armed resistance was anticipated. They were hard men with a hard code. Their task force had also suffered deaths and injuries, and the adrenaline was building up in them too. They had their orders: "Drug den, suspects thought to be armed, arrest." They were now standing silently by the garbage cans in the courtyard and waiting both on the staircase and in front of the apartment. It was too hot under their helmets and their riot masks. They were waiting for the word from the leader of the task force; everyone was eager to hear it now. At some point he would yell "Go, go, go" and then they'd do what they had been trained to do.

The old man at the window thought about Hassan and his friends. They had the key to his apartment and when they came during the night they made up the little packages in his kitchen, "stretching," they called it, two-thirds heroin, one-third Lidocaine. They compressed it into rectangular lumps with a jack. Each lump weighed a kilo. Hassan paid the old man a thousand euros every month, and he did it punctually.

Of course it was too much for one and a half rooms in the back of a building, fourth floor, too dark. But they wanted the old man's apartment; nothing served them better as their "bunker," as they called it. The kitchen was big enough and that was all they needed. The old man slept in the room and when they came he switched on the television so that he didn't have to listen to them. The only thing was, he couldn't cook any more: the kitchen was crammed with plastic wrappers, precision balances, spatulas, and rolls of adhesive tape. The worst thing was the white dust that settled in a film on everything. Hassan had explained the risk to the old man, but he didn't care. He had nothing to lose. It was a good business arrangement, and he'd never cooked anyway. He drew on his cigarette and looked up at the sky: not a cloud to be seen; it would get even hotter before evening.

Snow

He first heard the policemen when they broke down the door. It all went fast, and there was no point in fighting back. He was thrown to the floor, fell over the kitchen stool, and broke two ribs. Then they yelled that he was to tell them where the Arabs were. Because they were so loud, he said nothing. And also because his ribs hurt. He kept silent later in front of the examining magistrate too—he had been in prison too often, and he knew it was too early to talk. They wouldn't let him go now if he did.

———

The old man lay on his bed, cell number 178, C block, in the prison where detainees await trial. He heard the key and knew he had to say something to the female guard now, or nod, or move a foot; otherwise she wouldn't leave. She came every morning at 6:15; it was called "life check." They were looking to see if any of the prisoners had died in the night or killed themselves. The old man said everything was in order. The guard would also have collected his mail, but he had no one he could write to, and she no longer asked. When he was alone again, he turned to the wall. He stared at the bright yellow oil paint; the lower two-thirds of the walls were painted with it, then there was a white stripe. The floors were light gray. Everything here looked the same.

As soon as he woke up, he had thought about the fact that today was their wedding anniversary. And now he thought again about the man who was sleeping with his wife. His wife.

It had all started with the undershirt. He remembered

guilt

the summer evening twenty-two years ago when he found it under the bed. It was lying there all crumpled up and somehow dirty. It wasn't his undershirt, although that was what his wife kept saying. He'd known it belonged to the other man. After that nothing was the same. In the end he used it to clean his shoes, but that didn't change things either, and at a certain point he'd had to move out or else he'd have fallen apart. His wife cried. He didn't take anything with him; he left the money and the car and even the watch she'd given him. He quit his job. It was a good one, but he couldn't keep going there; he couldn't bear it any longer. He got drunk every evening, silently and systematically. At a certain point it became a habit, and he sank into a world of schnapps, petty crime, and social security. He didn't want anything else. He was just waiting for the end.

But today was different. The woman who wanted to talk to him was called Jana, plus a last name that had too many letters in it. They told him there had been a mix-up, she had applied for a visitor's permit. She didn't need his permission for that. So he went to the visitors' room at the appointed time and sat down with her at the table which was covered with green plastic. The officer who was supervising the conversation sat in the corner and tried not to disturb them.

She looked at him. He knew he was ugly. His nose and his chin had been growing towards each other for years until they almost formed a semicircle, his hair was almost all gone, and his stubble was gray. She looked at him anyway.

She looked at him in a way no one had looked at him for years. He scratched his neck. Then she said in a strong Polish accent that he had beautiful hands, and he knew she was lying, but it was okay that she said it. She was beautiful. Like the Madonna in the village church, he thought. As a boy he had always stared at her during Mass and imagined that God was inside her stomach, and that it was a riddle how he'd managed to get in there. Jana was in her seventh month; everything about her was round and radiant and full of life. She leaned over the table and touched his sunken cheek with her fingertips. He stared at her breasts and then was ashamed and said, "I've lost all my teeth." He tried to smile. She nodded in a friendly way. They sat at the table for twenty minutes and didn't utter another word. The officer was familiar with this; it often happened that prisoner and visitor had nothing to say to each other. When the officer said that visiting time was over she stood up, leaned forward quickly again, and whispered in the old man's ear, "Hassan is the father of my child." He smelled her perfume, and felt her hair on his old face. She blushed. That was all. Then she left and he was taken back to his cell. He sat on his bed and stared at his hands with their age spots and scars, he thought about Jana and the baby in her stomach, he thought about how warm and safe it was in there, and he knew what he had to do.

———

When Jana got home, Hassan was asleep. She undressed, lay down beside him and felt his breath on the back of her neck.

guilt

She loved this man whom she couldn't make sense of. He was different from the boys in her village in Poland, he was grown-up, and his skin seemed to be made of velvet.

Later, when he woke up for a moment, she told him the old man wouldn't testify against him; he could stop worrying. But he had to do something for him, buy him new teeth, she'd already spoken to a social worker who could take care of it. No one would find out. She was all worked up and talking too fast. Hassan stroked her stomach till she fell asleep.

———

"Does your client wish to make a statement about the men behind this? If so, the court could consider sparing him any further pretrial detention." I had taken on the defense on a pro bono basis and applied for a review of his remand. Everything had been negotiated with the court; the man would be released. It was not a complicated set of proceedings. The police had found two hundred grams of heroin in the apartment. Worse still: the old man had had a knife in his pocket. The law calls this "trafficking with a weapon"; the minimum sentence—the same as for manslaughter—is five years. The intention of the law is to protect officers from attack. The old man had to provide the name of the actual perpetrator: it seemed to be his only chance. But he remained silent. "In which case pretrial detention will continue," said the judge, shaking his head.

———

The old man was happy. The Polish girl must not have her baby alone. That's more important than me, he thought, and even as he was thinking it he knew that he'd won something distinct from—and more important than—his freedom.

———

The trial began four months later. They fetched the old man from his cell and led him to the courtroom. They had to pause for a moment in front of the Christmas tree. It was standing in the main corridor of the prison, as enormous as it was foreign, the electric candles reflected in the decorative balls which hung in orderly gradation, the largest ones at the foot, the smaller ones above. The electric cable from the bright red drum was attached to the floor with black-and-yellow warning stickers. There are safety precautions for things like that.

It rapidly became clear to the judges that the old man could not be the owner of the drugs; he simply didn't have the money for that. Nonetheless, what was at issue was the five-year minimum term. No one wanted to sentence him to something that high—it would have been unjust—but there seemed to be no way out.

During a recess something strange happened: the old man was eating some bread and cheese, which he was cutting with a plastic knife into tiny little pieces. As I was looking at him he apologized: he didn't have his teeth any more and had to cut up everything he ate into these little morsels. The rest of it was simple. That was why, indeed it was the only reason why, he had had the knife in his pocket. He needed it in order to be able to eat. There was a decision handed down by the Federal Court that said "trafficking with a weapon" didn't apply if the knife was clearly intended for another use.

The business with the teeth was perhaps an odd explanation, but this was also the last trial of the year. Everyone was relaxed, during the recesses the DA was talking about the presents he hadn't yet bought, and we were all wondering if it was going to snow. Finally the old man was given a two-year suspended sentence, and he was released from prison.

I wondered where he would spend Christmas; the lease on his apartment had been terminated and he had no one he could go to. I stood on one of the higher landings and watched him walk slowly down the stairs.

—

On the twenty-fourth of December, the old man was lying in the hospital. The operation wasn't due to take place until January 2, but the clinic had insisted that he go directly from jail to hospital. They were afraid of an alcoholic relapse. The social worker had organized everything, and when the old man was first told of it, he didn't want to do it. But then he heard that someone called Jana, or so the social worker said, had already paid for his new teeth at the clinic. Because they came from her he pretended she was a relative and agreed.

The hospital bed was clean, he'd showered and shaved, and they'd given him a gown with a yellow pattern on it. There was a Santa Claus made of chocolate on his nightstand. Its chest was squashed in and it looked oddly lopsided. He liked that. He's just like me, he thought. He was somewhat afraid of the operation; they were going to take a piece of bone from his hip. But he was excited about the new teeth. In a few months he would finally be able to eat normally again. As he went to sleep, he no longer dreamed of the undershirt under his bed. He dreamed of Jana, her hair, her smell, her stomach, and he was happy.

Just over a mile away Jana was sitting on the sofa telling her sleeping baby the Christmas story. She had cooked borscht for Hassan. It was a lot of work, but she knew how to do it; after her father died, that was how her mother had kept the little family's heads above water in Karpacz in southwestern Poland. Borscht made with brisket of beef and beets for the tourists who hiked over the mountain and were hungry. That had been her childhood, her mother standing out in the cold every day with her pots and her Bunsen burners among the other women, as they all squeezed the last of the goodness out of the vegetables and then threw them behind them into the snow. Jana told the baby about the red snow you could see from a long way away, and the fine smell of the soup and the gas burners. She thought about her village there in the mountains, and her family, and she told stories about Christmas, the yellow lights, roast geese, and Uncle Malek, who owned the bakery and certainly had baked the biggest cake again today.

Hassan was not coming back, she knew that. But he had been there with her when the baby came, he had held her hand and wiped the sweat from her forehead. He had stayed calm when she screamed, he was always calm when things came right down to it, and she believed nothing would happen to her as long as he was there. But she had also always sensed that he would go; he was far too young. She could only live in peace if she loved him from a distance. Suddenly she felt alone, she missed the village and her family, she missed it all so much it hurt, and she decided to take the train to Poland the next morning.

Hassan was driving through the city. He couldn't go see her; he didn't know what to say. He was engaged to another woman in Lebanon; he had to marry her, his parents had arranged it while he was still a child. Jana was a good woman; she had saved him from prison; she was clear and direct in every way. He slowly worked himself into a fury, at himself and his family and the world in general. And then he saw him.

The man was just coming out of a shop where he had been buying his last presents. He owed Hassan twenty thousand euros and had simply disappeared. Hassan had been looking for him for weeks. He stopped the car, took the hammer out of the glove compartment, and followed the man to the entrance of a building. Seizing him by the throat, he threw him against the wall. The shopping bags fell to the ground. The other man said he wanted to pay but it was taking a little time. He begged. Hassan wasn't listening to him any more; he was staring at the little gift parcels lying in the hallway. He saw the printed Father Christmases and the golden gift ribbons and suddenly it all came together in his head: Jana and the baby, the heat of Lebanon, his father and his future wife. He realized he couldn't change any of it now.

Snow

It took far too long and a neighbor said later he'd heard the blows interspersed with the screams, a dull, wet sound like you hear at the butcher's. When the police were eventually able to pull Hassan off the man's upper body, his victim's mouth was a mass of blood. Hassan had smashed eleven of his teeth with the hammer.

Snow did fall that night. It was Christmas.

—

The Key

The Russian spoke German with a heavy accent. The three of them were sitting on three red sofas in a café in Amsterdam. The Russian had been drinking vodka for hours while Frank and Atris drank beer. They couldn't work out the Russian's age, maybe he was fifty; his left eyelid drooped since his stroke, and his right hand was missing two fingers. He said he'd been a career soldier in the Red Army. "Chechnya and all that." He held up his mutilated hand. He liked talking about the war. "Yeltsin is a woman, but Putin, Putin's a man," he said. It was a market economy now, everyone understood that. A market economy meant you could buy anything. A seat in parliament cost $3 million, a ministerial post $7 million. Everything had been better during the war with Chechnya, and more honorable; men had been men. He had respected the Chechens. He'd killed a lot of them. Their children would already be playing with Kalashnikovs; they were good fighters, tenacious. They should drink to them. A lot of alcohol was drunk that evening.

They'd had to listen to the Russian for a long time. Finally he got around to the pills. Ukrainian chemists were going to make them; they'd lost their state jobs and were out of work. They'd had to privatize; their wives and children had to eat.

guilt

The Russian had also offered Frank and Atris everything imaginable: machine guns, howitzers, grenades. He'd even had a photo of a tank in his wallet. He'd looked at it tenderly and passed it around. He said he could get viruses too, but that was a dirty business. They all nodded.

Frank and Atris didn't want weapons. They wanted the pills. The previous night they'd tried out the drugs on three girls they'd taken along from a nightclub. The girls had told them in a mixture of English and German that they were going to study history and politics. They had all driven to the hotel, where they drank and fooled around. Frank and Atris had given them the pills. Atris found himself thinking repeatedly about the things they did next. The red-haired one had lain down on the table in front of Frank and tipped the ice from the champagne bucket on her face. She'd screamed it was too hot for her and they were to hit her, but Frank didn't want to. He had faced the table with his trousers down, smoking an enormous cigar, while his hips kept moving in the same rhythm and the girl's legs rested on his chest, as he kept up a complicated monologue about the dissolution of Communism and its consequences for the drug trade. The cigar made it hard to understand him. Atris lay on the bed and watched him. After he'd forbidden the two girls between his legs to keep going, they'd fallen asleep, one of them with his big toe still in her mouth. Atris realized the pills would be perfect for Berlin.

Now the Russian was talking about the drug-sniffing dogs. He knew everything about them. "In South Korea they even clone them because they're so expensive," he said. You had to weld a metal box into the car and then prepare it by stuffing bags of garbage, coffee, and wash powder into it, all separated by thick wrappers; it was your only chance to stop the dogs smelling something. Then he went back to talking about the war. He asked Atris and Frank if they'd ever killed anyone. Frank shook his head.

"With the Chechens it's like it is with potato chips," the Russian said.

"What?" said Frank.

"Potato chips. With the Chechens it's like with a bag of potato chips."

"I don't get it," said Frank.

"Once you start killing them, you can't stop till they're all gone. You have to kill them all. Every single one of them." The Russian laughed. Then suddenly he turned serious, and stared at his crippled hand. "Otherwise they come back," he said.

"Ah," said Frank. "The revenge of the chips . . . Now could we talk about the pills again?" He wanted to go home.

The Russian screamed at Frank: "You stupid asshole, why don't you listen? Look at your friend. He's a lump of meat but at least he's paying attention."

Frank looked over at Atris, who was sitting in the corner of the sofa. A dark blue vein was standing out on his forehead. Frank knew that vein, and knew what was going to happen next.

"We're talking about the war here, and you don't have time to listen? We can't do business this way. You're idiots," said the Russian.

Atris stood up. He weighed 230 pounds. He lifted one side of the glass table until it was on edge. Bottles, glasses, and ashtrays landed on the floor. He went for the Russian, who was faster than they'd expected and sprang to his feet, pulling a pistol out of his waistband and pressing the muzzle to Atris's forehead.

"Easy, my friend," he said. "This is a Makarov. It makes big holes, big ones, better than those American toys. So sit down or there's going to be one hell of a mess."

Atris's face had flushed a deep crimson. He took a step back. The mouth of the pistol had left a white mark on his forehead.

"So. Sit down again. We have to drink," said the Russian. He summoned a waiter. They sat down and started drinking again.

It would be a good piece of business. They would make a lot of money and there would be no problems. They just had to pull themselves together, thought Atris.

There was a bus stop opposite the café. Nobody noticed the woman waiting on the bench. She had pulled the hood of her black sweater over her head; in the darkness she was hard to distinguish from her surroundings. She didn't get into any of the buses. She seemed to be asleep. Only when Atris leapt to his feet did she open her eyes for a moment. Otherwise she didn't move.

Atris and Frank didn't notice her. They also didn't see the Russian give her a brief signal.

The Key

———

Atris stood on the balcony of the apartment on the Kurfürstendamm looking out for the dark blue Golf. It was drizzling. Frank would be back from Amsterdam in twenty-four hours and they would have the new designer drugs, better than anything on the market. The Russian had said he would give them the pills on commission. They would have three weeks to pay him the 250,000 euros.

Atris turned round and went back into Frank's apartment. It was built in the classic old Berlin way: twelve-foot ceilings, moldings, parquet floors, five rooms. They were almost empty. Frank's girlfriend was an interior designer. She'd said, "The spaces have to work." Then she'd had the sofas and chairs and everything else taken out. Now everyone had to sit on gray felt cubes with tiny backs. Atris found it uncomfortable.

Before he left, Frank had told Atris what he had to do. His instructions had been clear and very simple. Frank always spoke clearly and simply to him. "It's not hard, Atris, you just have to listen really carefully. First: Don't let the key out of your sight. Second: Keep an eye on the Maserati. Third: Only leave the apartment when Buddy has to shit." Buddy was Frank's mastiff. Frank made him repeat it. Five times. "Key, Maserati, Buddy." He wouldn't forget. Atris admired Frank. Frank never made fun of him. He'd always told him what he had to do and Atris had always done it. Always.

guilt

_____

When he was fourteen, Atris had been the weakest boy in his class, and in Wedding the weakest got beaten up. Frank had protected him. Frank had also got him his first anabolic steroids; he'd said they'd make Atris strong. Atris didn't know where Frank got the stuff. When he was twenty, the doctor diagnosed liver damage. His face was covered with pustules and oozing lumps. When he was twenty-two, his testicles had almost disappeared. But Atris had become strong in the meantime, nobody beat him up any more, and he didn't believe the rumors that anabolic steroids come from cattle breeding.

Today he was going to watch some DVDs, drink beer, and go out with the mastiff now and then. The Maserati was downstairs in the underground parking garage. The key to the locker was on the kitchen table. Frank had written it all down on a piece of paper. "6 p.m. Feed Buddy." Atris didn't like the huge animal; it always looked at him in such a peculiar way. Frank had once said he'd given Buddy steroids too, something had gone wrong, and the animal just wasn't the same as he'd been before. Everyone thought Atris was dumb, but nothing was going to go wrong for him this time.

He went back into the empty living room and tried to switch on the Bang & Olufsen TV. He sat down on a felt cube and took a long time to work out how to use the remote. Atris was proud that he was the one Frank had entrusted with his apartment, his dog, and the locker in the new main station. He picked up a joint from the table and lit it. They were going to be rich, he thought. He would buy his mother a new kitchen, the one with the double-wide range he'd seen in a high-end decorating magazine of Frank's girlfriend's. He blew a smoke ring and sucked it right back in again. Then he put his feet on the table and tried to follow the talk show.

The dog food consisted of pieces of beef chopped up small; the bowl was on the kitchen table. The mastiff was lying on the black-and-white-tiled floor. It was hungry. Smelling the meat, it got up, growled, and then began to bark. Atris dropped the remote in the living room as he ran to the kitchen. He got there too late. The mastiff had pulled the tablecloth to the floor. The chunks of flesh were flying through the air in a sticky clump, and Atris saw the mastiff go up on its hind legs, mouth open, waiting. Suddenly something glinted amidst the bits of meat and it took a mere fraction of a second for Atris to understand. He screamed, "Out . . ." and leapt from his position in the doorway. The mastiff was quicker. It didn't so much as look at him. The mass of meat landed in the dog's jaws with a smack. It didn't even chew; it just swallowed. Atris skidded across the floor and hit the wall in front of the dog. The dog licked the flagstones clean. Atris yelled at him, yanked open his mouth, and looked into his maw, got him in a headlock and throttled him. The dog growled and snapped at him. Atris wasn't fast enough; the dog got his left earlobe and tore it off. Atris slammed his fist against the dog's muzzle, then sat on the floor, his blood dripping on the flagstones and his shirt torn. He stared at the dog and the dog stared back. Frank hadn't been gone for more than two hours and he'd already screwed things up: the dog had swallowed the key to the locker.

———

They almost beat him to death. It was an oversight.

Once past the border, Frank had been followed by members of a special task force. He needed to use the toilet so he drove to a rest stop. The leader of the task force was nervous. He made the wrong decision and gave the order for an arrest. Later the state police had to reimburse the owner of the gas station for both broken washbasins, the lock on the toilet door, the door itself, which had been smashed in, the air dryer, and the cleanup. They put a sack over Frank's head, dragged him out of the toilet, and took him to Berlin. He had put up a fight.

The woman in the hoodie had been following Frank's Golf since he left Amsterdam. She had watched the task force with a little pair of binoculars. Once everything was over, she used a phone booth to call the number of a stolen cell phone in Amsterdam. The conversation lasted twelve seconds. Then she went back to her car, typed an address into the GPS unit, pushed back the hood of her sweater, and drove onto the Autobahn again.

———

Atris waited eight hours to see if the dog would spit the key out again. Then he gave up and dragged Buddy down into the street. The rain had started coming down more heavily in the meantime, the dog got wet, and when he finally got into the Maserati, it stank up the car. He would have to clean the upholstery later, but first he needed the key.

The vet had said on the phone that he had to come. Atris started the car. He was in a rage. He gave it too much gas, and the car shot out of the parking space, its right wing making contact with the bumper of the Mercedes in front of it with a metallic sound. Atris got out, cursing, to look at the scrape in the paintwork. He tried polishing the damage with his finger but a splinter of the lacquer tore his skin and he started bleeding. Atris gave the Mercedes a kick, got back in the car, and drove off. The blood on his finger stained the pale leather on the steering wheel.

The vet's offices were on the ground floor of a building in Moabit. The blue sign outside said SMALL ANIMAL PRACTICE. Atris couldn't read very well. After he'd deciphered the sign, he wondered if Buddy qualified as a small dog. He hauled the beast out of the car onto the street and gave him a kick in the backside. Buddy snapped at him but missed. "Filthy monster, you small animal," said Atris. He didn't want to wait, so he yelled at the nurse. She let him jump the queue because he was making too much noise. When he got into the examination room, he put a thousand euros in fifty-euro notes on the vet's steel table.

"Doctor, this damn fucking dog swallowed a key. I need the key but I need the dog too. Cut the beast open, get the key out, then close him up again," said Atris.

"I have to x-ray him first," said the vet.

"I don't give a fuck what you do. I need the key. I have to leave. I need the key and the damn dog."

"You can't take him with you if I cut him open. He'll need to lie flat, undisturbed, for at least two days. You have to leave him here."

"Open him up, and he's coming with me afterwards. He's tough: he'll survive," said Atris.

"No."

"I'll give you more money," said Atris.

"No. Money won't heal the dog."

"Crap," said Atris. "Money heals everything. I'm not giving the money to the damn dog, I'm giving it to you. You open him up, you take the key out, you close him up again. You take the money. Everyone goes home happy."

"It's impossible. Please try to understand. It's simply impossible—no matter how much money you give me."

Atris paced up and down the examination room and thought. "Okay. Next possibility. Can the damn dog just shit the key out again?"

"If you're in luck, yes."

"Can you give him something to make him shit quicker?"

"You mean a laxative? Yes, that could work."

"Right. So how stupid are you anyway? Why do I have to explain everything to you? You're the doctor. Give him the stuff to make him shit. A lot, enough to work on an elephant."

"You have to give him natural laxatives. Liver, lungs, or udders."

"What?"

"It helps."

"Are you out of your mind? Where am I going to get udders? I can't set the dog on a cow to rip off her udders." Atris looked at the nurse's tits.

"You can get these things at the butcher's."

"Give him a pill. Now. You're a doctor. You give people pills. A butcher gives people udders. Everyone has their own job. Do you get it?"

The vet didn't want any more argument. The week before, he'd had a letter from the bank to say that he needed to balance his account. There were a thousand euros lying on the table. In the end he gave the mastiff Animalax, and because Atris put another two hundred euros on the table, the dose was five times what was recommended by the manufacturer.

Atris dragged Buddy out into the street again. The rain was sheeting down. He cursed. The vet had said the dog needed to be kept moving; it would make the medicine work quicker. He had no desire to get wet, so he jammed the lead into the passenger door and drove off slowly. The dog trotted along beside the Maserati. Other cars honked. Atris turned the music up louder. A policeman stopped him. Atris said the dog was sick. The policeman yelled at him, so he pulled the mastiff into the car and drove on.

At the next corner he heard it. It was a dark, ominous rumbling. The mastiff suddenly opened its jaws, panted, howled in pain, then voided itself. It hunched over in the front seat, forced its rear end backwards and up between the armrests, bit into the upholstery, and tore out a large mouthful. The liquid shit sprayed over the seats, the windows, and the hat rack. The dog spread it around with its paws. Atris braked and leapt out of the car, closing the driver's door. It lasted twenty minutes. Atris stood in the rain while the car windows steamed up from inside. He kept getting glimpses of the dog's nose, its red gums, and its tail, he heard its high-pitched yowling, and waves of shit kept hitting the windows. Atris thought about Frank. And about his father, who'd told him while he was still a child that he was too stupid even to walk in a straight line. Atris thought that maybe his father had been right.

———

Frank woke out of the coma in the prison hospital in Berlin. The task force had overdone it: he had a severely fractured skull, bruises all over his body, and they'd broken his collarbone and his upper right arm. The examining magistrate read him the warrant at his bedside; the only charges were resisting arrest and bodily harm—one of the eight officers had had his little finger broken. The police had found no drugs, but they were convinced these must be somewhere.

I took over his defense. Frank would remain silent. The DA's office would have a hard time proving drug trafficking. The custody hearing was in thirteen days' time, and if nothing new turned up, he would be set free.

———

"You stink of shit," said Abdul.

Atris had called him. Before that he had searched the Maserati for an hour, and his shirt and pants were smeared with it. He hadn't found the key; it must still be inside the mastiff. Atris hadn't known what to do. Abdul was his cousin; in the family he was rated as intelligent.

"I know I stink of shit. The car stinks of shit, Buddy stinks of shit, I stink of shit. I know that. You don't have to say it."

"Atris, you *really* stink of shit," said Abdul.

Abdul did business out of one of the countless converted spaces under the arches of the Berlin suburban railway. The railroad company rented out these spaces. There were auto body shops, storerooms, and junk dealers. Abdul recycled old tires. He got paid to get rid of them, loaded them onto a truck, and threw them into a ravine he'd discovered in a forest in Brandenburg. He earned good money. Everyone said he was a talented businessman.

Atris told Abdul about the thing with the dog. Abdul said he should bring Buddy inside. The mastiff looked wretched, and its white coat was all brown.

"The damn dog stinks too," said Abdul.

Atris groaned.

"Tie him to the steel post," said Abdul.

He showed Atris the shower in the back room, giving him a freshly washed set of coveralls from the city garbage collectors. It was orange.

"What's this?" said Atris.

"I need it for the recycling work," said Abdul.

Atris undressed and packed his old things into a garbage bag. Twenty minutes later when he came out of the shower, the first thing he saw was the jack, lying in a pool of blood. Abdul was sitting on a chair, smoking. He pointed to the body of the dog on the floor.

"Sorry, but you'd better get undressed again. If you cut him open, you'll get a mess all over you again. That's the last clean set of coveralls."

"Shit."

"It's the only way. The key would never have come out—it's caught in his stomach. We'll get another dog."

"And the Maserati?"

"I've already made a phone call. The boys are going to steal another one, exactly the same model. We just have to wait. You'll get the new one."

———

Atris came back to the apartment on the Kurfürstendamm at two o'clock in the morning. He had parked the new Maserati in the underground parking garage. It looked completely different; it was red, not blue, and the seats were black instead of beige. It was going to be hard to explain to Frank.

Atris took the elevator up. The key seemed to stick a little in the door of the apartment, but he was too tired to notice. He couldn't fight back; he didn't even try. The woman was petite, she was wearing a hoodie, and he couldn't see her face. Her pistol was enormous.

"Open your mouth," she said. Her voice was warm.

She shoved the barrel between Atris's teeth. It tasted of oil.

"Walk backwards slowly. If you make a false move or I stumble, the back of your head will blow off, so you'd better be careful. Do you understand?"

Atris nodded carefully. Inside his mouth, the bead on the barrel struck his teeth. They went into the living room.

"I'm going to sit down on the stool. You are going to kneel in front of me. Very slowly." She was talking to him the way a doctor talks to a patient. The woman sat on one of the felt cubes. Atris knelt down next to her. He still had the barrel in his mouth.

"Very good. Now if you do everything right, nothing's going to happen. I don't want to kill you, but it doesn't matter to me whether I do or not. Do you understand?"

Atris nodded again.

"So, I'm going to explain it to you."

She spoke slowly, slowly enough for Atris to understand it all, and leaned back on the stool, crossing her legs. Atris had to follow her movements and bend his head forward.

"You and your partner bought pills from us. You want to give us 250,000 euros for them. Your partner was arrested on the Autobahn. We're sorry about that. But you still have to pay the money."

Atris swallowed. Frank got caught, he thought. He nodded. She waited till she could be sure Atris had got it.

"I'm glad you understand. Now I'm going to ask you a question. After I'm done, you can take the barrel out of your mouth so you can answer. When you've finished answering, you put the barrel back in your mouth. It's quite simple."

Atris was getting used to the voice. He didn't have to think. He was just going to do everything the voice said.

"Where is the money?" she said.

Atris opened his mouth and said: "The money's at the station. Buddy swallowed the key, he shat all over everything, I had to . . ."

"Quiet," said the woman. Her voice was sharp. "Put the barrel back in your mouth immediately."

Atris stopped talking and did as he was told.

"Your story's too long. I don't want to listen to a whole novel. All I want is to know where the money is. I'm going to ask you again. I want you to answer in a single sentence. You can take your time to work out the answer. When you know what you want to say, open your mouth and say the sentence. But only one sentence. If you say more than one sentence, I'll cut your balls off. Do you understand?"

Her voice hadn't changed. Atris began to sweat.

"Where is the money?"

"In a locker in the main station," said Atris, and immediately bit down on the steel again.

"Very good, now you've got it, this is exactly the way it goes. Now comes the next question. Think about it, open your mouth, say one sentence, and shut it again. Work out your answer. So, here's the question. Who has the key to the locker?"

"Me," said Atris and closed his mouth again.

"Do you have it here?"

"Yes."

"I'm proud of you. We're getting somewhere. Now comes the next question. Where is your car?"

"In the parking garage."

"I see we're getting on with each other. Now it gets a little more complicated. Here's what we're going to do. You're going to stand up, but you're going to do it very slowly. Do you understand? What matters is doing it all really slowly.

The Key

We don't want the thing to go off because I get scared. If we're careful, nothing's going to happen."

Atris slowly got to his feet. He still had the pistol in his mouth.

"I'm going to take it out of your mouth now. Then you're going to turn round and walk to the door. I'm behind you. We're going to drive together to the station now. If the money is there, you can go."

Atris opened his mouth and she pulled out the barrel.

"Before we go, there's one thing you need to know. There are special cartridges in the pistol. They contain a drop of nitroglycerin. You're going to walk ahead of me. If you run, I'll have to shoot. The nitroglycerin will explode in your body. There will be nothing left of you that anyone can recognize. Do you understand?"

"Yes," said Atris. Nothing would make him run.

They took the elevator down. Atris went ahead and opened the door to the parking garage. Someone yelled, "That's the pig." The last thing Atris saw was the metal baseball bat. It shone red.

―――――

They'd stolen the wrong Maserati. The car belonged to a rapper. He'd been having dinner with his girlfriend in Schlüterstrasse. Afterwards, when he couldn't find his car, he'd called the police, but the car hadn't been towed away. His girlfriend got in a bad mood. She wound him up till he called his old friends from Kreuzberg. Muhar El Keitar promised to take care of it.

_____

If you didn't belong to the police, it wasn't hard to find out who now had the car. El Keitar was the head of a large family. They all came from the same village, and they were Lebanese Kurds. El Keitar wanted the car. He made that clear. His friend the rapper was a famous man now, and he absolutely wanted to help him. The four men who paid Abdul a visit on Muhar El Keitar's orders didn't want to kill him; all they wanted to know was who the car had been for. But something went wrong. When they came back, the men said Abdul had tried to fight back. He'd said where the car was, but then it was all over.

_____

When Atris regained consciousness, he was on a wooden chair, bound and naked. It was a damp, windowless room. Atris got scared. Everyone in Kreuzberg had heard of this cellar. It belonged to Muhar El Keitar. Everyone knew that El Keitar liked to torture people. They said he'd learned the technique during the war in Lebanon. There were a lot of stories about it.

"What's going on?" Atris asked the two men who were sitting on a table in front of him. His tongue was all furred and swollen. Between his legs was a car battery with two cables.

"Wait," said the younger man.

"What am I waiting for?"

"Just wait," said the older one.

The Key

Ten minutes later Muhar El Keitar came down the stairs. He looked at Atris. Then he screamed at the two men.

"I've told you a thousand times you're to put the tarp under the chair. Why don't you ever get it? Next time I won't say anything and you can see how you get all the shit cleaned up."

In fact, Muhar El Keitar didn't want to torture people. That sentence was almost always enough to get his victims to talk.

"What do you want, Muhar?" asked Atris. "What should I do?"

"You stole a car," said El Keitar.

"No, I haven't stolen any car. The boys stole it. The other Maserati was full of shit."

"Good, I understand," said El Keitar, although he didn't understand at all. "You have to pay for the car. It belongs to a friend."

"I'll pay."

"And you'll pay compensation for my costs."

"Of course."

"Where's your money?"

"In a locker in the main station." Atris had learned in the meantime that there was no sense in telling long stories.

"Where's the key?" asked Muhar El Keitar.

"In my wallet."

"You're morons," Muhar El Keitar said to the two men. "Why didn't you check it? I have to do everything myself." El Keitar went over to Atris's orange garbage company coveralls. "Why do you have garbage company overalls?" said Muhar El Keitar.

"It's a long story."

Muhar El Keitar found the wallet and inside it the key.

"I'm going to the station myself. You guys keep an eye on him," he said to his men, and then to Atris: "If the money's there, you can go."

He went back up the stairs. Then he came down again backwards. He had a pistol in his mouth. El Keitar's two men reached for the baseball bats.

"Put them down," said the woman with the pistol.

Muhar El Keitar nodded vigorously.

"If we all stay calm, nothing's going to happen to anyone," said the woman. "We're going to solve our problems together."

————

Half an hour later Muhar El Keitar and the older of his two men were sitting on the floor of the cellar, bound to each other with zip ties. Their mouths were sealed with parcel tape. The older one still had his undershorts on; Atris was now wearing his clothes. The younger one was sitting in a huge pool of blood. He'd made a mistake and pulled a blackjack out of his pocket. The woman's pistol had still been in El Keitar's mouth. With her left hand she'd pulled a switchblade out of the front pocket of her hoodie, opened it, and plunged it deep into the inner part of his right thigh. It was over quickly: he registered almost nothing. He had dropped to the floor at once.

"I severed your femoral artery," she said. "You're going

to bleed out, it'll take six minutes. Your heart will keep pumping the blood out of your body. Your brain will be the first to go; you'll lose consciousness."

"Help me," he said.

"Now for the good news. You can survive. It's simple. You have to reach into the wound and find the end of the artery. Then you have to squeeze it shut between your thumb and your forefinger."

The man looked at her in disbelief. The pool of blood was getting bigger.

"If I were you, I'd get a move on," she said.

He'd groped around in his wound. "I can't find it, dammit, I can't find it." Then the bleeding suddenly stopped. "I got it."

"Now you can't let go. If you want to live, you have to stay sitting down. At some point a doctor will get here. He'll close off the artery again with a little steel clip. So keep still."

And to Atris she said, "Let's go."

———

Atris and the woman drove to the main station in the stolen Maserati. Atris went to the locker and opened it. He set down two bags in front of the woman and opened them.

"How much money is that?" she asked.

"Two hundred and twenty thousand euros," said Atris.

"And what's in the other one?"

"One point one kilos of cocaine," said Atris.

"Good. I'll take both. The thing is all settled. I'm leaving now, you'll never see me again, and you've never seen me," she said.

guilt

"Yes."

"Repeat it."

"I've never seen you," said Atris.

The woman turned, picked up both bags, and headed for the escalator. Atris waited for a moment or two, then ran to the nearest phone booth. He picked up the receiver and dialed the police emergency number.

"A woman in a black hoodie, just under five feet tall, slim, is in the main station, heading for the exit." He knew how the police talk. "She's armed, she's carrying a bag of counterfeit money and a kilogram of cocaine. She's stolen a blue, no, a red Maserati. It's in parking garage number two," he said and hung up.

He went back to the locker and reached into it. Behind the coin slot—invisible from the outside—a second key was taped. He used it to open the next-door locker and took out a bag. He looked into it for a moment. The money was still there. Then he went back into the main hall and took the escalator up to the suburban train platforms. Down at the lowest level he saw the woman lying on the ground, surrounded by eight policemen.

Atris took the first train to Charlottenburg. As it came in, he leaned back. He had the money. Tomorrow the big package from Amsterdam with the pills in it would reach his mother. Frank had even included a windmill in the package that lit up red and green. She loved things like that. The post office didn't have drug-sniffing dogs yet, the Russian had said; they cost too much money.

The Key

The woman would be sentenced to four or five years. The cocaine was admittedly only sugar, but Frank and Atris had once fallen for the counterfeit money trick themselves. Aside from which, there was still possession of a weapon and the theft of a car.

Frank would be set free in a few days; nothing could be proved against him. The pills would find a ready market. When Frank got out, he'd give him a puppy, or definitely a smaller dog. They had saved 250,000 euros, and the woman's arrest was the Russian's problem: these were the rules. Frank would be able to buy himself the new four-door Maserati.

After he'd told me the whole story, Atris said, "You just can't trust women."

Lonely

Today she walked past the house again for the first time in a long time. It had all happened fifteen years ago.

She sat down in a café and called me. Did I remember her? she asked. She was a grown-up now, with a husband and two children. Both girls, ten and nine years old, pretty children. The younger one looked like her. She didn't know who else to call.

"Do you still remember it all?" she asked.

Yes, I still remembered it all. Every detail.

———

Larissa was fourteen. She lived at home. The family's only income was from welfare; her father had been out of work for twenty years, her mother had once been a cleaning lady, and both drank. Her parents often came home late. Sometimes they didn't come home at all. Larissa had gotten used to this, and to the beatings, the way children get used to anything. Her brother had moved out when he was sixteen and never been heard from again. She was going to do the same.

It was a Monday. Her parents were in the corner liquor store. That's where they were almost always to be found.

guilt

Larissa was alone in the apartment, sitting on the bed, listening to music. When the bell rang she went to the door and peered through the peephole. It was her father's friend Lackner, who lived next door. She was wearing nothing but a T-shirt and panties. He asked where her parents were, came into the apartment, and checked that she really was alone. Then he pulled the knife. He told her to get dressed and come with him or he'd slit her throat. Larissa obeyed; there was nothing else she could do. She went with Lackner, who wanted to be in his apartment where no one could disturb him.

Frau Halbert, the neighbor who lived in the apartment across the hall, was coming up the stairs towards them. Larissa tore herself free, screamed, and ran into her arms. Much later, when it was all over, the judge would ask Frau Halbert why she hadn't protected Larissa. Why she had detached herself from Larissa's embrace and had left her to Lackner. The judge would ask her why she had watched as the man took the girl away although she was begging and crying. And Frau Halbert would always answer in the same way. To every question she replied, "It wasn't my business; it was nothing to do with me."

Lackner took Larissa to his apartment. She was still a virgin. When he had finished, he sent her home. "Say hi to the old guys" were his farewell words. Back in the apartment, Larissa took a shower under such hot water that it almost scalded her skin. She closed the curtains in her room. She was in pain, she was terrified, and there was no one she could tell.

In the next few months things went badly for Larissa. She was tired, she threw up, and she couldn't concentrate. Her mother said she shouldn't eat so much candy, it caused her heartburn. Larissa gained almost twenty pounds. She was in the middle of puberty. She had only just taken down the pictures of horses from her wall, and hung up photos from teen magazines. Things got worse, particularly the pains in her stomach. "Colic," said her father. Her periods had stopped coming: she thought it was because of the revulsion.

On the twelfth of April she barely made it to the toilet. She thought her bowels would explode—she'd had cramps in her stomach all morning. It was something else. She reached between her legs and felt something strange that was growing out of her. She touched sticky hair and a tiny head. "It mustn't be inside me," she said later. This had been her only thought, over and over again: It mustn't be inside me. A few minutes later the baby dropped down into the toilet bowl; she heard the water splash. She stayed sitting. She lost all track of time.

At some point she stood up. The baby was lying down there in the toilet bowl, white and red and greasy and dead. She reached up to the shelf above the washbasin, took the nail scissors, and cut the umbilical cord. She dried herself off with toilet paper but she couldn't throw that on top of the baby, so she stuffed it into the plastic bucket in the bath, then sat on the floor till she got cold. When she tried to walk, she wobbled, but she fetched a garbage bag from the kitchen, supporting herself against the wall and leaving a bloody handprint. She pulled the baby out of the toilet, its tiny legs as thin as her fingers. She laid it on a towel. She looked at it, a brief look that was far too long; it lay there, its face blue and its eyes closed. Then she folded the towel over the baby and pushed it into the bag. Carefully, like a loaf of bread, she thought. She took the bag down to the cellar, carrying it with both hands, and set it between the bicycles, weeping silently. On the steps back up she began to bleed. It ran down her thigh, but she didn't notice. She made it as far as the apartment, then collapsed in the hall. Her mother, who had come home, called the fire department. In the hospital the doctors took care of the afterbirth and alerted the police.

The policewoman was friendly; she wasn't in uniform, and she stroked the girl's forehead. Larissa lay in a clean bed; one of the nurses had brought her a few flowers. She told them everything. "It's in the cellar," she said. And then she said something that no one could believe: "I didn't know I was pregnant."

I visited Larissa in the women's prison. A judge who was a friend of mine had asked me to take her on as a client. She was fifteen. Her father gave an interview to the tabloids, saying she'd always been a good girl and he just couldn't understand it. He was paid fifty euros.

Lonely

There have always been repressed pregnancies. Every year in Germany alone, 1,500 women recognize too late that they're pregnant. And year after year, almost 300 women only realize it when they give birth. They misinterpret all the signs: menstruation has ceased because of stress, the stomach is distended because of overeating, the breasts are enlarging as a result of some hormonal disturbance. These women are either very young or over the age of forty. Many have already had children. People can repress things, though nobody knows how the mechanism works. Sometimes it's totally successful: even doctors are deceived and refrain from further physical exams.

Larissa was set free. The presiding judge said the child had been born alive, it had drowned, its lungs had been fully developed, and coliform bacteria had been found in them. He said he believed Larissa. The rape had traumatized her and she hadn't wanted the child. She had repressed everything so powerfully and so completely that she literally had no knowledge of her pregnancy. When she had delivered the baby on the toilet, she had been astonished. As a result, she was in a state in which she could no longer distinguish right and wrong. She was therefore not guilty of the death of the newborn infant.

In a separate trial, Lackner was sentenced to six and a half years.

Larissa took the streetcar home. All she had with her was the yellow plastic bag that the policewoman had packed for her.

guilt

Her mother asked how it had been in court. Larissa moved out six months later.

———

After our phone conversation she sent me a photo of her children. She also included a letter, written in her best copy-book handwriting on blue paper; she must have done it very slowly. "Everything is fine with my husband and my girls. I'm happy. But I often dream about the baby lying alone in the cellar. It was a boy. I miss him."

Justice

The criminal court is in the Moabit district of Berlin. That part of the city is gray; no one knows where the name came from; it sounds a little like the Slavic word for a Moor. It is the largest criminal court in Europe. The building has twelve courtyards and seventeen staircases. Fifteen hundred people work here, including 270 judges and 350 prosecutors. Approximately 300 hearings take place every day, 1,300 prisoners from 80 nations are incarcerated here awaiting trial, and more than 1,000 visitors, witnesses, and trial personnel pass through. Every year roughly 60,000 criminal proceedings are handled here. These are the statistics.

The officer who delivered Turan said quietly that he was "a poor bastard." He arrived in the interrogation room on crutches, dragging his right leg. He looked like the beggars in the pedestrian passageways. His left foot was turned inward. He was forty-one years old, a thin little man, just skin and bones, sunken cheeks, almost no teeth, unshaved, unkempt. In order to shake my hand, he had to lean one of the crutches against his stomach, and he found it hard to keep his balance. Turan sat down and tried to tell me his story. He was serving his term of detention; the sentence had long since started to run. He had supposedly attacked a man with his pit bull, and "brutally beaten him up and kicked him." Turan said he was innocent. It took time for him to answer my questions, and he spoke slowly. I didn't understand everything he said, but then he didn't have to say much: he could barely walk, and any dog would have knocked him over. When I was about to leave, he suddenly clutched my arm, and his crutch fell to the ground. He wasn't a bad man, he said.

A few days later the file arrived from the DA's office. It was thin, barely fifty pages. Horst Kowski, forty-two, had gone for a walk in Neukölln. Neukölln is a district of Berlin where schools employ private guards, technical schools have up to 80 percent foreign pupils, and every second person is on welfare. Horst Kowski had gone for this walk with his dachshund. The dachshund had gotten into a fight with the pit bull. The owner of the pit bull got angry, the fight escalated, and the man assaulted Kowski.

When Kowski arrived home, he was bleeding from the mouth. His nose was broken, his shirt badly torn. His wife bandaged him up. She said she knew "the man with the pit bull" and his name was Tarun. He was a regular at the tanning salon where she worked. She checked the computer in the salon, and found Tarun's discount card and his address: Kolbe-Ring 52. The couple went to the police; Kowski showed them the computer printout. Tarun was not a registered resident of Berlin. The officer was not surprised:

Neukölln is not a place where the obligation to register is always observed.

The next day the officer on the beat failed to find any Tarun among the 184 names on the little signs next to the buzz-ers at Kolbe-Ring 52. There was, however, a label with the name "Turan." The policeman made inquiries at the State Residents' Registration Office; there was in fact a Harkan Turan registered at Kolbe-Ring 52. The officer thought it must be a misspelling—it should be Turan, not Tarun—so he rang, and when no one answered he left a summons for Turan in the mailbox.

Turan didn't go to the police. Nor did he send an excuse. After four weeks the policeman sent the file to the DA's office. The DA requested a penalty order and a judge signed it. If he didn't do it, he'll surface, he thought.

When Turan received the order he could still have changed everything; all he had to do was write one line to the court. The penalty order took on the force of law after two weeks. The department in charge of enforcement sent a form for a money transfer to use when he paid the fine. He naturally didn't pay because apart from everything else, he didn't have the money. The fine was replaced by a term of imprison-ment. The detention center wrote telling him to present himself within fourteen days. Turan threw the letter away. After three weeks two policemen came to get him in the morning. Since then he had been sitting in prison. Turan said: "It wasn't me. Germans are so thorough—they must know this."

guilt

Turan's deformity was congenital; he'd had a whole series of operations. I wrote to his doctors and gave their case notes to an expert in the field. He said Turan was incapable of assaulting anyone. Turan's friends came to my office. They said he was afraid of dogs so of course he'd never owned one. One of the friends even knew Tarun and his pit bull. I demanded that the matter be reopened. Turan was released. Three months later there was a hearing. Kowski said he'd never seen Turan in his life.

Turan was exonerated. The court forgot about the charge against Tarun.

By law, Turan had a claim against the state: eleven euros for every day of wrongful imprisonment. The claim had to be made within six months. Turan didn't get any money—he missed the deadline.

Comparison

Alexandra was pretty: a blonde with brown eyes. In older photographs she wears a hair band. She grew up in the country near Oldenburg, where her parents were livestock farmers: cows, pigs, hens. She didn't like having freckles, she read historical novels, and all she wanted was to go and live in the city. After middle school, her father got her an apprenticeship in a respectable bakery and her mother helped her look for an apartment. At first she felt homesick and went home on weekends. Then she got to know people in the city. She loved life.

After she'd completed her apprenticeship she bought her first car. Her mother had given her the money, but she wanted to choose it herself. She was nineteen. The salesman was ten years older. Tall, slim-hipped. They took a test drive, and Thomas explained the points of the car to her. She was drawn to his hands: slender, sinewy, they attracted her. Afterwards he asked her if she would like to have dinner with him, or go to a movie. She was too nervous, so she laughed and said no. But she wrote her phone number on the contract. They made a date a week later. She liked the way he talked about things. And she liked it that he told her what to do. Everything felt right.

They married two years later. In her wedding photographs she's wearing a white dress. She's tanned, she's laughing into the camera and holding the arm of her husband, who's a couple of heads taller. They had paid for a real photographer. The picture was to stand on her night table forever: she'd already bought the frame. They both liked the reception afterwards, and the solo entertainer on the Hammond organ; they danced, although he said he was not much of a dancer. Their families got on well together. Her favorite grandfather, a stonemason with silicosis, gave them a statue as a wedding present—a naked girl who looked a lot like her. His father gave them money in an envelope.

Alexandra had no worries; everything was going to work out well with this man. It was all the way she'd wished it for herself. He was loving, and she thought she knew him.

———

The first time he hit her was long before the baby was born. He came home drunk in the middle of the night. She woke up and told him he smelled of alcohol. She didn't find it that bad; she was simply telling him. He yelled at her and dragged the bedclothes off her. As she sat up, he hit her in the face. She was terrified; she couldn't say a thing.

Next morning he wept and blamed the alcohol. She didn't like the way he sat on the kitchen floor. He said he would never drink again. When he left for work, she cleaned the entire apartment. She did nothing else all day. They were married, she thought; that sort of thing happened, it was a slip-up. They didn't discuss it again.

When Alexandra got pregnant, everything became the way it had been before. He brought her flowers on weekends, he lay on her stomach and tried to hear the baby. He stroked her. When she came home from the hospital after the birth, he had tidied everything up. He'd painted the nursery yellow and bought a baby's changing table. Her mother-in-law had brought new things for the child. There was a wreath of paper flowers over the door.

The girl was baptized. He'd wanted to name her Chantal, but finally they settled on Saskia. Alexandra was happy.

After the birth he didn't have sex with her any more. She tried a few times, but he didn't want it. She felt a little lonely, but she had the baby and she made herself get accustomed to it. A girlfriend had told her it sometimes happened if the husband had been present at the birth. It would pass. She didn't know if this was true.

———

After a few years, things got harder. Sales of cars were slow; they had the payments on the apartment to make. They managed somehow, but he drank more than in former times. Sometimes in the evenings she smelled a perfume she didn't know, but she didn't say anything. Her friends had bigger problems with their husbands; most of them were getting divorced.

guilt

_____

It began at Christmas. She had set the table: white cloth, her grandmother's silver. Saskia was five; she said where the balls were to be hung on the Christmas tree. At half past six Alexandra lit the candles. He still wasn't home by the time they had burned all the way down. The two of them were alone, and after dinner she put Saskia to bed. She read aloud from the new book till the little girl fell asleep. She had phoned her parents and his parents and everyone had wished one another Merry Christmas like a normal family. Only when they asked about him, Alexandra said he was making a quick trip to the gas station to buy matches, because she had none in the house for lighting the candles.

He did it silently. He had boxed when he was younger and knew how to hit in order to cause pain. Although he was drunk, his blows were precise. He struck systematically and hard, as they stood in the kitchen between the American breakfast counter and the refrigerator. He avoided her face. On the refrigerator door were the little girl's paintings and stickers. Thinking of Saskia, she bit into her hand so as not to scream. He dragged her across the floor to the bedroom by her hair. When he sodomized her, she felt she was being torn in half. He came almost at once, then kicked her out of bed and fell asleep. She lay on the floor, unable to move, until at some point much later she managed to make it to the bathroom. The bruises were already showing on her skin and there was blood in her urine. She lay in the bathtub for a long time, until finally she was able to breathe normally again. She was unable to cry.

The first day after the Christmas holidays she found the necessary strength to say she was taking Saskia and going to her mother's. He left the apartment before she did. She packed a suitcase and carried it to the elevator. Saskia was excited. As they arrived downstairs, he was standing in front of the door. He took the suitcase out of her hand gently. Saskia asked if they weren't going to visit Grandma after all. Taking their daughter in his left hand and the suitcase in his right, he went back to the elevator. In the apartment he laid the suitcase on the bed, looked at her, and shook his head.

"No matter where you go, I'll find you," he said. In the hall, he picked Saskia up in his arms. "We're going to the zoo."

"Yes, yes!" said Saskia.

It was only after the door closed that Alexandra could feel her hands again. She had dug her fingers into the chair so tight that two of her fingernails were broken. That evening he broke one of her ribs. She slept on the floor. She was devoid of feeling.

———

His name was Felix and he'd rented one of the small apartments in the back of the building. She had seen him every day with his bicycle, he always said hello to her in the supermarket, and when she buckled over in the hallway once with pain in her kidneys, he'd helped with her shopping bags. Now he was standing at her door.

guilt

"Do you have any salt?" he said. "Okay, I admit it, that's a really stupid line. Would you like to have coffee with me?"

They both laughed. Her ribs hurt. She had gotten used to the blows: she would stick it out for another four or five years, then Saskia would be old enough. She was nine now.

She liked Felix's apartment. It was warm, with pale floors, books on narrow shelves, and a mattress with white sheets. He talked to her about books and they listened to Schubert lieder. He looks like an overgrown boy, she thought, and maybe a little sad. He told her she was beautiful, then neither of them said anything for a long time. When she went back to her apartment, she thought that perhaps her life wasn't over after all. She had to spend that night on the floor by the bed again, but it didn't matter quite so much.

Three months later she slept with him. She didn't want him to see her naked, with the blue patches and all the scraped skin, so she lowered the metal blinds and undressed under the bedcovers. She was thirty-one, he didn't have much experience, but for the first time since Saskia's birth a man was really making love to her. She liked the way he held her. Afterwards they lay in the dark room. He talked about the trips he would like to take with her, about Florence and Paris and other places she'd never been. It all seemed so simple to her; she liked the sound of his voice. She could only stay for two hours. She told him she didn't want to go back; she said it just like that, it was a declaration of love, but then she realized that she actually meant it.

Later she couldn't find her stockings, which made them laugh. Suddenly he switched on the light. She clutched the sheet up to her body, but it was too late. She saw the fury in his eyes; he said he was going to call the police, it had to be done at once. It took her a long time to dissuade him, telling him she was afraid for her daughter. He didn't want to understand. His lips were trembling.

————

The summer holidays began two months later. They took Saskia out to her grandparents' in the country; she loved it there. On the trip back to the city Thomas said, "Now you're really going to learn obedience." Felix sent her a text message saying he missed her. She read it in the toilet at the rest stop on the Autobahn. It stank of urine in there, but it made no difference to her. Felix had said her husband was a sadist who enjoyed humiliating and hurting her. It was a mental disturbance, it could be dangerous for her, and her husband needed treatment. She had to leave, and at once. She didn't know what to do. She was too ashamed to tell her mother, ashamed for him and ashamed for herself.

————

August twenty-sixth was the last day before Saskia came back. They were going to pick her up and spend the night. Then the three of them were going to Majorca; the tickets were on the table in the hall. She thought things would go better there. He had drunk a great deal during Saskia's absence. She could barely walk. In the past two weeks he had subjected her to anal and oral rape every day, he had beaten her, and he had forced her to eat out of a bowl on the floor. When he was there she had to be naked; she slept on the floor in front of his bed; he had also now confiscated the bedclothes. She hadn't been able to see Felix. She'd written to tell him it was simply impossible.

During this last night he said, "Saskia's ready now. She's ten. I've waited. When she comes back, she's going to be mine."

She didn't understand what he was saying, and asked him what he meant.

"I'm going to fuck her the way I fuck you. She's ready."

She screamed and flew at him. He stood up and hit her in the stomach. It was a short, hard blow. She vomited, he turned round and told her to clean it up. An hour later he went to bed.

———

Her husband was no longer snoring. He'd always snored, even during the first night, when they were happy. At the beginning it had been strange; another human being, she had thought, another voice. Gradually she had gotten used to it. They had been married for eleven years now. There would not be a second life, there was only this man and this life. She sat in the other room, listening to the radio. They were playing a piece she didn't know. She stared into the darkness. In two hours it would be getting light and she'd have to go over into the bedroom, their bedroom.

———

Her father asked me to defend his daughter. I got a visitor's pass. The DA in charge was named Kaulbach, a solidly built, plainspoken man who talked in short sentences.

"Horrifying business," he said. "We don't get many murders. This one's an open-and-shut case."

Kaulbach showed me the photos of the crime scene.

"She beat her husband to death with a statue while he was asleep."

"Whether he was asleep or not is something the medical examiner can't determine," I said, knowing that this wasn't a strong argument.

The problem was simple. Manslaughter does not distinguish itself from murder by degree of "intent" the way you see it in crime dramas on TV. Every murder is a manslaughter. But it's also more. There has to be some additional element that makes it a murder. These defining elements are not arbitrary: they are laid out in the law. The perpetrator kills "to satisfy sexual urges," out of "greed" or out of other "base motives." There are also words to define *how* he kills, for example "heinously" or "brutally." If the judge believes such a defining element is present, he has no choice: he must give the perpetrator a life sentence. If it's manslaughter, he has a choice; he can sentence the perpetrator to anywhere between five and fifteen years.

Kaulbach was right. When a man is battered to death in his sleep, he cannot defend himself. He is unaware that he is being attacked; he's helpless. The perpetrator is thus acting with malice. He is committing murder, and will receive a life sentence.

"Look at the pictures," said Kaulbach. "The man was lying

on his back. There are no defensive wounds on his hands. The bedclothes on top of him aren't disturbed. There was no struggle. There can be no doubt: he was asleep."

The DA knew what he was saying. It looked as if the base of the statue had been stamped into the man's face. The blood had sprayed everywhere, even onto the photo on the night table. The jury was not going to like these images.

"And moreover your client confessed today."

I hadn't been made aware of this until now. I had to ask myself what I was doing in this case. I wouldn't be able to help her.

"Many thanks," I said. "I'm going to visit her now. We can talk again after that."

———

Alexandra was in the prison hospital. She smiled, the way you smile at a stranger who visits you on the ward. She sat up and put on a bathrobe. It was too big for her; she looked lost in it. The floor was covered with linoleum, everything smelled of disinfectant, and one of the edges of the washbasin had broken off. Next to her was another woman; their beds were only separated by a yellow curtain.

I sat in her room for three hours. She told me her story. I arranged for her broken body to be photographed. The medical report ran to fourteen pages: spleen and liver ruptured, both kidneys crushed, large areas where blood had pooled under the skin. Two cracked ribs; six others with evidence of previous fractures.

———

Comparison

The trial began three months later. The presiding judge would be retiring shortly. Gaunt face, crew cut, gray hair, rimless glasses—he didn't look as if he belonged in the new courtroom. An architect had designed it in contemporary style with bright green plastic molded chairs and white Formica tables. It was supposed somehow to represent democratic justice, but it didn't have any effect on the sentences being handed down. The presiding judge called the court to order and established that all parties in the trial were present. Then he ordered a halt in the proceedings while the public was asked to leave and Alexandra was taken back to the holding cell. He waited till everything was quiet.

"I'm speaking to you openly, ladies and gentlemen," he said. His voice was slow; he sounded tired. "I don't know what we should do. We will proceed with the trial and we will make sure that we comprehend the files. I do not wish to condemn the accused; she has suffered under this man for ten years, and he almost killed her. And his next act would probably have been to assault the child."

I didn't know what I should say. In Berlin the DA's office would have had the judge removed immediately for bias; such candid comments at the beginning of a trial would be unthinkable. But out here in the provinces it was different. People lived closer together, and everyone had to get on with one another. The presiding judge didn't care what the DA thought, and Kaulbach stayed sitting quite calmly.

"I will have to sentence her, the law gives me no choice," he said. He looked at me. "Unless of course something occurs to you. I will give you every latitude."

The trial indeed lasted only two days. There were no witnesses. Alexandra told her story. The medical examiner testified about the autopsy of the victim and, at greater length, about Alexandra's injuries from the abuse. The hearing of evidence took place in closed court. The DA argued that it was murder; he spoke without emotion and there was no way to find fault with his presentation. He said that the defendant met all the conditions that would apply with a less serious charge. But in cases of murder the law offered no possibility of mitigation of sentence; that was how it had been drafted. Thus the only appropriate verdict was a life sentence. My address to the jury was scheduled for the following day. Until then the court was adjourned.

Before we left the courtroom, the presiding judge asked the DA and me to approach the bench. He had taken off his robe. He was wearing a green jacket; his shirt was frayed and covered with stains.

"You're wrong, Kaulbach," he said to the DA. "No, there isn't any lesser charge in cases of murder, but there are other possibilities." He handed each of us some Xeroxed sheets. "Study the decision before tomorrow. I would like to hear some sensible arguments from you." That last remark was directed at me.

I was familiar with the decision. The Federal Supreme Court had ruled that the sentence in cases of murder is not absolute. Even a life sentence can be commuted in certain exceptional cases. That was the argument I used in my summing up; I didn't have any other ideas.

The court set Alexandra free. The presiding judge said she had acted in self-defense. It's a difficult rule. In order to be allowed to defend yourself, an attack must be either in progress or imminent. You cannot be punished for defending yourself. The only problem was that a sleeping man cannot instigate an attack. And no court had ever accepted that an attack is imminent when the attacker is asleep. The presiding judge said it was a unique decision, an exception; it was valid only in this one instance. Alexandra had not been obliged to wait until he woke up. She had wanted to protect her daughter, and she was permitted to do so. She herself had been in fear of her life. The court lifted the order of arrest and released her from detention. Later the judge persuaded the DA not to appeal.

———

After the decision was announced, I went to the café on the opposite side of the street, where you can sit outside under an enormous chestnut tree. I thought about the old presiding judge, the hasty trial, and my stupid address to the jury: I had prayed for a mild sentence and she had been declared not guilty. It suddenly occurred to me that we hadn't heard from any fingerprint experts. I checked the files in my laptop: no traces had been found on the statue. The perpetrator must have worn gloves. The statue weighed ninety pounds, Alexandra barely weighed that herself. The bed was almost two feet off the ground. I read her statement once again. She said that after she'd done it, she'd sat in the nursery until first light, then she'd called the police. She hadn't showered and she hadn't changed her clothes. Roughly one hundred pages further on in the file were the photos of her clothes: she had been wearing a white blouse. There was no trace of blood on it anywhere. The presiding judge was experienced. There was no way he could have overlooked it. I closed the screen. It was late summer, the very last days, and the wind was still warm.

I saw her coming out of the courthouse. Felix was waiting for her in a taxi. She got into the backseat with him. He took her hand. She was going to go with him to her parents', take Saskia in her arms, and it would all be over. They would have to be very careful with each other. Only when she felt the warmth in her stomach would she reciprocate, squeezing the hand that was squeezing hers and had killed her husband.

Family

Waller graduated from school with the highest marks of anyone in Hannover. His father was an ironworker, a little man with drooping shoulders. He had managed somehow to make sure his son qualified for the elite high school, although his wife had run away, abandoning the boy. Sixteen days after Waller passed his exams, his father died. He slipped and fell into the freshly poured foundation of a new building. He had a bottle of beer in his hand. They couldn't stop the machine in time, and he drowned in the liquid concrete.

Besides Waller, four of his father's workmates attended the funeral. Waller wore his father's only suit, which fit him perfectly. He had his father's square face and his thin lips. Only his eyes were different. And everything else.

The German Scholarship Fund offered Waller a grant, but he turned it down. He bought a ticket to Japan, packed a suitcase, and traveled to Kyoto, where he entered a monastery for twelve months. In the course of the year he learned Japanese. After that he applied for a job with a firm of German mechanical engineers in Tokyo. Five years later he became head of the branch. He lived in a cheap boardinghouse. All the money he earned went into an investment account. A Japanese carmaker hired him away. After six years he had reached the highest position that a foreigner had ever held there. He now had approximately two million euros in his account, he was still living in the boardinghouse, and he had spent almost nothing at all. He was thirty-one years old. He resigned and moved to London. Eight years later he'd made almost thirty million on the stock exchange. In London, too, all he had was one tiny room. When he turned thirty-nine, he bought a manor house on a lake in Bavaria. He put all his money into bonds. He didn't work any more.

A few years ago, I rented a small house on this lake for three weeks in the summer. You could see the manor house through the trees; there was no fence between the two properties. I met Waller for the first time on the dock in front of my house. He introduced himself and asked if he might sit down. We were roughly the same age. It was a hot day, we put our feet in the water, and we watched the dinghies and colorful windsurfers. It didn't bother us that neither of us said much. After two hours, he went back home.

The next summer, we arranged to meet in the lobby of the Frankfurter Hof. I arrived a little late; he was already waiting. We had coffee; I was tired after a day at trial. He said I must come back soon; every morning herons, a great flock of them, flew over the lake and the house. Finally, he asked me if he might send me a file.

It arrived four days later, and was the story of his family, compiled by a detective agency.

Waller's mother had married again a year after the divorce, and had given birth to another son, Waller's half brother, Fritz Meinering. When Fritz Meinering was two, the new husband left his family. The mother died of alcohol poisoning as the boy was starting school. Meinering ended up in a children's home. He wanted to become a carpenter. The home found him a place as an apprentice. He began drinking with friends. It wasn't long before he was drinking so much that he couldn't make it to work in the mornings. He was fired, and he left the children's home.

After that the crimes began: theft, bodily harm, traffic offenses. He spent two brief periods in jail. At the Oktoberfest in Munich, he drank enough to produce a blood alcohol level of 3.2. He insulted two women and was sentenced for public drunkenness. He spiraled down, lost his apartment, and started sleeping in homeless shelters.

A year after the incident at the Oktoberfest, he held up a grocery store. All he said to the judge was that he'd needed the money. He'd still been so drunk from the night before that the salesgirl was able to knock him down with a dustpan. He got two and a half years in prison. He went into a treatment program for alcoholics, which earned him early release.

For a few months he succeeded in staying sober. He found a girlfriend. They moved in together. She worked as a salesclerk. He was jealous. When she came home too late one night, he hit her over the ear with a saucepan lid and the eardrum burst. The judges sentenced him to another year.

Fritz Meinering got to know a drug dealer in prison, a week before they were released. The man persuaded Meinering to carry cocaine from Brazil to Germany. His airfare would be covered, plus he'd be paid five hundred euros. The police were tipped off and he was arrested in Rio de Janeiro in a taxi on the way to the airport. There were twelve kilos of uncut cocaine in the trunk. He was sitting in prison there, awaiting trial.

This was where the file ended. After I'd read it all, I called Waller, who asked me if I could organize his half brother's defense in Brazil. He didn't want any personal contact with him, but he felt he had to do this. He asked me to fly there, arrange for lawyers, talk to the embassy, and take care of everything. I agreed.

———

The prison in Rio de Janeiro had no cells, just barred cages with narrow pallets. The men sat there with their feet pulled up, because the floor was wet. Cockroaches ran over the walls. Meinering was completely unkempt. I told him that a man who wished to remain anonymous had paid for his defense.

I hired a sensible defense lawyer. Meinering was sentenced to two years. After that he was sent home for trial in Germany. Because a year of prison in Brazil, given the catastrophic conditions, is calculated as the equivalent of three

years of jail time in Germany, his trial was called off and he
was released.

Three weeks later he got into a fight with a Russian in a bar
over a half bottle of vermouth. Both of them were drunk
and the barkeeper threw them out. There was a building site
in front of the bar. Meinering got hold of a construction
worker's lamp and hit the other man over the head with it.
The Russian collapsed. Meinering wanted to go home. He
lost his sense of direction and kept walking along the fence
bordering the site until he'd rounded it completely; twenty
minutes later he was back in front of the bar. In the meantime the Russian had crawled some distance, bleeding. He
needed help. The lamp was still lying on the ground. Meinering picked it up and kept hitting the Russian until he was
dead. He was arrested at the scene.

———

Next time I was in Munich, I drove out to visit Waller.

"How do you want to proceed?" I asked.

"I don't know," he said. "I don't want to do any more for
him."

It was a brilliantly sunny day, with the light glinting off
the yellow house and its green shutters. We were sitting
down at the boathouse. Waller was wearing beige shorts and
white canvas shoes.

"Wait a moment, I'm going to fetch something." He went
up to the house. A young woman was lying out on the ter-
race. The lake was almost as flat as a mirror.

Waller came back and handed me a photo.

"That's my father," he said.

It was a Polaroid from the 1970s. The colors had faded at some point and now it was tinged brownish yellow. The man in the picture looked just like Waller.

"He was in prison four times," he said. "Three for fights that he started, and once for theft. He'd taken money from the till."

I handed back the photo. Waller put it in his pocket.

"His father was condemned to death in 1944 by the Nazis for raping a woman," he said.

He sat down on one of the chairs and looked out at the lake. Two dinghies were having a race; the blue one seemed to be winning. Then the red one came about and gave up. Waller stood up and walked over to the grill.

"We can eat soon. Will you stay?"

"Gladly," I said.

He poked around with a fork in the glowing heat.

"Better to leave nothing after we're gone," he said suddenly. That was all.

His girlfriend came down to us and we talked about other things. After we'd eaten he accompanied me to my car. A lonely man with a thin mouth.

A few years later there was a report in the newspaper that Waller had died; he'd slipped off his boat in a storm and drowned. He left his money to the monastery in Japan and his house to the local Bavarian church on the lake. I had liked him.

Secrets

The man came to our offices every morning for two weeks.
He always sat in the same place in the big conference room.
Mostly he held his left eye shut. His name was Fabian Kalk-
mann, and he was mad.

In our very first conversation, he said the secret services were
after him. Both the CIA and German Intelligence. He knew
which secret they wanted. This was the way things were.

"They're hunting me, do you understand?"

"Not completely, so far."

"Were you ever in the stadium during a soccer match?"

"No."

"You have to go. They all call my name. They call it all the
time. They yell Mohatit, Mohatit."

"But your name is Kalkmann," I said.

"Yes, but the secret services call me Mohatit. It's what I'm
called in the Stasi files too. Everyone knows that. They want
my secret, the big one."

Kalkmann leaned forward.

"I went to the optician. For my new glasses, you know.
They drugged me, through my eye. I came out of the eye-

glasses store exactly one day later, exactly twenty-four hours later."

He looked at me.

"You don't believe me. But I can prove it. Here," he said, pulling out a little notebook, "here, take a look. It's all in here."

In big capital letters it said in the notebook 26.04, 15 hundred hours, enter lab. 27.04, 16 hundred hours, exit lab. Kalkmann closed the notebook again and looked at me triumphantly.

"So, now you've seen it. That's the proof. The eyeglasses store belongs to the CIA and German Intelligence. They drugged me and took me to the cellar. There's a big laboratory down there, a James Bond laboratory all built of high-grade steel. They operated on me for twenty-four hours. That's when they did it." He leaned back.

"Did what?" I asked.

Kalkmann looked around. He was whispering now. "The camera. They inserted a camera in my left eye. Behind the lens. Yes—and now they see everything I see. It's perfect. The secret services can see everything that Mohatit sees," he said. Then he raised his voice. "But they won't get my secret."

Kalkmann wanted me to bring charges against German Intelligence. And the CIA, of course. And former American president Reagan, who was responsible for the whole thing. When I said Reagan was dead, he replied, "That's what you think. He's actually living up in the attic at Helmut Kohl's house."

Secrets

He came every morning to tell me about his experiences. At a certain point I'd had enough. I told him he needed help. It was amazing: he saw reason at once. I called the emergency psychiatric services and asked if I could come by with a patient. We took a taxi. We had to go to the locked criminal unit because the other rooms were in the course of being painted. The bulletproof glass doors closed behind us; we went deeper and deeper into the building, following a male nurse. Finally we were seated in an anteroom. A young doctor I didn't know asked us to come into his consulting room. We sat down in the visitors' chairs in front of a small desk. I was about to explain things when Kalkmann said:

"Good day, my name is Ferdinand von Schirach, I'm a lawyer." He pointed at me. "I'm bringing you Mr. Kalkmann. I think he has a severe problem."

A NOTE ABOUT THE AUTHOR

Ferdinand von Schirach was born in Munich in 1964. Since 1994, he

has worked as a criminal defense lawyer in Berlin. Among his clients

have been the former member of the Politburo Günter Schabowski,

the former East German spy Norbert Juretzko, and members of the

underworld.

A NOTE ABOUT THE TRANSLATOR

Carol Brown Janeway's translations include Bernhard Schlink's *The Reader*, Jan Philipp Reemtsma's *In the Cellar*, Hans-Ulrich Treichel's *Lost*, Zvi Kolitz's *Yosl Rakover Talks to God*, Benjamin Lebert's *Crazy*, Sándor Márai's *Embers*, Yasmina Reza's *Desolation*, Margriet de Moor's *The Storm*, and Daniel Kehlmann's *Measuring the World, Me and Kaminski*, and *Fame*.

A NOTE ON THE TYPE

This book was set in Mrs. Eaves, a typeface designed in 1996 by Zuzanna Licko and modeled after the work of John Baskerville but named for Sarah Eaves, who became Baskerville's wife after the death of her first husband.

Zuzanna Licko (b. 1961) is a cofounder of Emigre, a pioneer digital type foundry.

Typeset by Scribe, Philadelphia, Pennsylvania

Printed and bound by RR Donnelley, Harrisonburg, Virginia

Book design by Robert C. Olsson